LOV

Rick circled the plane, checking to see that everything was in order. He was wearing gray cords and a forest green turtleneck that complemented his deeply bronzed skin. I noticed that although he wasn't overly muscular, there was a certain strength about him.

If I weren't so in love with Brad Matthews, I thought, I could definitely find Rick Gillian intriguing—that is, if he didn't have such an irritating personality. Just then, he turned to face me and caught me totally off guard with a question.

"Did you get all of that?" he asked, referring to his inspection and explanation of preflight precautions.

"Ah—uh—yes," I stammered.

"And did everything look right to you?"

I took a chance and said, "Everything looks fine to me." Then I added, "But I'm not the authority, am I?"

"Right. On both counts," Rick replied in a stern voice. Then he smiled. I couldn't help myself; I was smiling back.

Bantam Sweet Dreams Romances
Ask your bookseller for the books you have missed

Love Is In The Air

Diana Gregory

BANTAM BOOKS

TORONTO • NEW YORK • LONDON • SYDNEY • AUCKLAND

RL 6, IL age 11 and up

LOVES IS IN THE AIR
A Bantam Book / December 1985

Cover photo by Pat Hill

ISBN 0-553-25245-3

Published simultaneously in the United States and Canada

Bantam Books are published by Bantam Books, Inc. Its trademark, consisting of the words "Bantam Books" and the portrayal of a rooster, is registered in U.S. Patent and Trademark Office and in other countries. Marca Registrada. Bantam Books, Inc., 666 Fifth Avenue, New York, New York 10103.

Printed and bound in Great Britain by Hunt Barnard Printing Ltd.

O   0 9 8 7 6 5 4 3 2 1

Special Thanks

I would like to say a special thank you to Gary Phillips of the South Lake Tahoe Flying Club for helping to refresh my memory on the ups and downs of flying a small plane.

Chapter One

"You actually won?" Patty turned and stared at me, eyes wide, as she shoved through the swinging doors of the cafeteria.

"Ummm . . . yeah." I shrugged and followed her. We joined the line in front of the steam tables. Taking a tray off the top of the pile, I set it on the rails. "I guess."

"You *guess*!"

"Uh-huh." I paused, looking at the macaroni and cheese and the fried halibut, then moved on to the sandwich section.

"This incredible thing happens to you and you only *guess*?" Patty insisted.

I picked up one of the plastic-wrapped triangles and checked to see what it was. Tuna. I put it on my tray along with a bag of chips.

"Have you told Brad?"

"Uh—" I picked up a carton of milk.

"Well?"

Brad Matthews. Tall with dark blond, straight hair, he had serious gray eyes that made my heart race each time I looked into them, even after we'd been going steady for four months. "No." I dug into my purse for money to pay the cashier. I handed it to her, then picked up my tray. "I haven't had time."

"Oh, sure!" Patty's voice was edged with sarcasm. "He only drove you to school this morning, two whole miles, and you couldn't find the time to say, 'Hey, Brad, guess what? I've just won ten flying lessons'? Deena, who are you trying to kid? This is me, your best friend from way back in the sixth grade. Get real, huh?"

I looked at the carton of chocolate milk Patty was holding. "Is that all you're getting?"

"Yes," she answered impatiently. "Well? What about Brad?"

"I think we're blocking the way," I said. "Do you see a table anywhere?"

She looked around, "Yes, over there."

We wound our way to a spot against the far wall. Slipping into one of the seats, I asked, "Why just the milk? That's not your style."

"No real time to eat." Patty shook the carton, then opened it and popped in a straw.

"I'm meeting Richard in a couple of minutes. I made a mess out of the math assignment due next period. He promised to do it over for me."

"Good thing he's so wild for you," I said, smiling. "With your math anxiety, you'd better not break up with him until graduation."

"You're right." Patty smiled back briefly. She pushed a stray lock of reddish-blond hair away from her face. "But about the raffle—I still can't get over the fact you won first prize. There must've been thousands of tickets sold."

"And I bought my share," I said, thinking how I'd wanted to surprise Brad. Now I couldn't.

"Then why aren't you leaping madly around and shouting the news to the world? I sure would be."

I sighed as I tore open the plastic wrap on my sandwich. "See, I bought the tickets with the idea of winning second prize, not first. I wanted the portable typewriter, not the flying lessons." I took a small bite. After I swallowed it, I said, "What am I supposed to do with flying lessons?"

"What are you supposed to do with a portable typewriter?" Patty looked confused. "You don't know how to type."

"Well, I decided it was time I learned."

"Why? If you're going to be an artist, you'll never need it."

"Promise you won't laugh?"

"I promise." She held up one hand, swearing.

"I'd thought I could earn some money typing up other students' assignments. You know, it would be like a small business."

"Wait a second. I know—I can see it all now. You did this to please Brad, didn't you? Since you didn't take those dull, boring business classes he wanted you to take this semester, you decided to prove to him you could still be businesslike." She nodded. "Am I right, or am I right?"

"I was only trying to be practical," I insisted.

"Like old Brad, huh? And buying all those raffle tickets was really being practical? No wonder you don't want to tell him." Patty shook her head. "Deena, you're unbelievable. Why don't you stop trying to turn yourself into a Brad Matthews clone? Just be yourself again. Please! If you don't, I swear you're going to end up with a split personality." She shook her head again. "I barely know you now. You're beginning to act like someone going on forty-five instead of eighteen. With orthopedic shoes, yet!"

I glanced down at my new pink Sportos. "Hardly!"

"I meant that figuratively." Patty looked exasperated. "All I know is that I liked the fun, adventurous pre-Brad Deena a lot more. *She* would have loved those flying lessons."

I looked down at my sandwich for a minute. Then I looked back up and said casually, "I thought you were supposed to be meeting Richard any minute?"

"You're changing the subject," Patty accused me.

"Right." I nodded. "We're friends, and I want to stay that way."

"It's just that—"

"Do I say things about Richard?" I asked.

"What's there to say about Richard, except that he's adorable and romantic . . ." she said, her voice trailing off.

"And never on time," I interjected.

"But he *is* romantic!" Patty looked smug. "That's more than I can say for Brad, the senior voted most likely to bore you to sleep."

"That's *the senior voted most likely to succeed*," I said in an even tone. "And I thought we were going to drop the subject."

"That was you, not me." Patty sighed. "Oh, Deena, it's only because I *am* your best friend, I worry about you." Reaching across the table, she squeezed my hand affectionately. Then she looked up and waved. "There's Richard at last." She began gathering up her books and purse. "I've got to go, Deena. I'll talk to you later."

"But not," I warned, "on the subject of boyfriends."

"OK, I promise." Patty stood up, and there was a friendly twinkle in her eyes as she added, "At least for now." Her voice turned serious. "But, Deena, do me a favor, please? Don't go trying to give away those flying lessons, or exchange them for the typewriter, or for something else you think is supposed to be practical."

Patty took a breath and continued. "Why not use the lessons, huh? You know what I think? I think it's fate telling you that you need some excitement, something new in your life."

"But Brad—"

"I thought that we'd dropped the subject of boyfriends." Then, before I could think up a proper reply, she'd waggled her fingers in a friendly wave and said, "Ciao!"

I sat down on the low stone wall by the parking lot, wiggled my toes inside my shoes, then pulled my feet up and wrapped my arms around my legs. The spot was my usual place to wait for Brad, and I intended to take advantage of the warm, early-spring sun. I closed my eyes, resting my chin on my knees. Brad would be awhile yet. It was his business club meeting day, and he was always the last to leave, waiting to ask the adviser some question.

The day was the combination of warm and cool that marks the beginning of spring in Pinebrook. Our town is located in the lower foothills of the Sierra Nevada Mountains, on the Nevada side. Above the town are the snow-capped peaks that surround Lake Tahoe. Sometimes people ski up there into May, long after everyone in Pinebrook has begun to wear shorts. That's the cool part, the breezes that slip down the sides of the Sierras. The warm part comes from the desert valley below us. Actually, a lot of it has been turned into farms. From Pinebrook you can look out over the valley and see the water sparkling in the irrigation canals. So I guess it would be safe to say that Pinebrook has the best of both the mountains and the desert.

It was on a warm spring day the week before that I'd had an idea for a picnic. When I'd first suggested it to Brad, he hadn't seemed very interested. But I had assured him it would be special. It would be this next Saturday, and I knew the weather would be perfect. I planned to borrow Mom's wicker hamper, then fill it with french bread, a selection of cheeses, and grapes to feed each other—one by one. It would be very romantic. I'd have to wear jeans to be practical, but that didn't mean I couldn't wear a pretty blouse. Maybe my pink peasant one with the white eyelet and the dark pink ribbons.

I realized I'd used the word *practical* and remembered the conversation Patty and I had had at lunch and how she'd accused me of becoming too practical.

It had been almost spooky the way Patty had told me not to exchange the flying lessons for something useful, like the typewriter. Because that was exactly what I'd been planning on doing. In fact, I'd decided to call the boy who'd won the typewriter as soon as I got home from school to see if he'd consider a trade. If he would, I'd be able to tell Brad about my idea for learning to type.

Patty was wrong to think that I needed some kind of excitement in my life. I had Brad. He was more than enough. Patty just couldn't understand that not everyone wanted a boyfriend like Richard Lewis. He acted as if the world were a big amusement park and not serious the way Brad knew it was.

The Sunday before, Patty and I had been sitting on her front lawn when Richard had come roaring down the street on his motorbike, a cloud of colored balloons streaming behind him. He'd swerved wildly into the drive, halted in front of her, then untied the balloons from the handlebars and presented them to her with an elaborate bow. When I'd told Brad about Richard, he'd reminded me of how dangerous it had been for Richard to drive through traffic that way. I loved Brad all the more for his maturity.

I shifted to a position facing away from the sun, then put my head down again. Another thing wrong with Richard was that he could never be counted on to get anywhere on time. He was always late, sometimes forgetting to show up at all. Brad could always be counted on to be prompt, and he'd never forget to meet me somewhere. So what if he'd never think of bringing me a bouquet of balloons?

"Hey, Deena, wake up."

I jumped, my eyes flying open. Brad was standing in front of me. He wasn't alone. "I wasn't asleep," I insisted, though my voice did sound thick.

"Deena, you know Tabitha Wingford, don't you?" Brad motioned toward the girl standing beside him.

"Uh—oh, hi," I said, swinging my feet off the top of the wall in order to stand up. Without having to look down, I knew my shirt was

9

no longer tucked neatly into the waistband of my skirt. But I wasn't about to stand there tucking it in. Not in front of tall, slender, always perfectly groomed Tabitha Wingford. Just being near her made me feel even dumpier than my five-foot-two-inch, one-hundred-and-ten-pound frame. Oh, I knew Tabitha Wingford. Who in school didn't? She was one of those girls involved in every school activity, a member of every committee formed—if not the head of it.

"And you know Deena, don't you?" Brad asked Tabitha.

"Of course." She smiled at me. "You did the posters for our Halloween charity drive, didn't you? They were very good."

"Thank you." I smiled back.

We looked at each other for a long moment. Then she raised a slim hand and swept back an abundance of long, silky blond hair from her shoulder. Turning to Brad, she said, "Well, I'd better be going." She touched the large folder he was carrying under one arm, her delicately painted pink nails doing a light tattoo on the cover. "You're welcome to keep these if you want." Then her hand touched his arm, and it lingered a lot longer than necessary, I thought, before she let it drop to her side. I pretended not to notice.

"Hey, thanks," Brad said, patting the

folder in the same place where her hand had been. "It's my first real shot at spread-sheet printouts."

"Spread sheets?" I asked feeling slightly out of it. No one heard me.

"Anytime," Tabitha said sweetly.

"I'm going home right now to work up a new set of figures," Brad added.

"You do that," Tabitha said and smiled as if there were some kind of private joke between them. Then she turned to me. "It was nice talking to you, Donna."

"It's Deena," I corrected. But she was already walking toward a bright yellow Toyota parked nearby.

After she'd taken about ten steps, though, she stopped and turned back. "And don't forget about Saturday," she called lightly.

"Don't worry!" Brad called back. "I won't."

I waited until she'd tucked her long legs into the shiny new car and started the motor before I said, "Saturday?"

"Oh, yeah!" Brad said enthusiastically. We started to walk toward his car. "Tabitha's father bought her a personal computer. That's how we got on the subject of spread sheets. It's one of the programs that came with the computer. And since we were discussing their application in business at the club meeting

11

today, she was nice enough to invite me over to run some figures on Saturday."

"But, Brad—"

Tabitha had circled the lot by this time and was driving slowly past us. She waved.

"What?" Brad asked absently, waving back.

"Our picnic!"

"Our—" I could see the confusion mirrored in his eyes. Then suddenly he came to a halt and slapped his forehead with one hand. "Our picnic!" He frowned. "Oh, Deena, I really am sorry. For a minute there I actually had forgotten." Brad was looking remorseful. "It's only that you know how much I want a computer. And to have the chance to get my hands on one for an entire afternoon, well—" He shrugged, his shoulders adding apology.

We'd reached his car. Standing together before getting in, I could see the two of us reflected in the window. His face below the shock of dark blond hair was so honest, so open, so handsome. Beside his image, nearly a whole head lower, was mine, scowling. My small features were pinched in the center of a cloud of dark, shoulder-length hair. The only bright thing I could see about myself was my turquoise blouse. I changed my frown into a smile. Turning, I looked sweetly up at him and accepted his apology. "It's all right," I said softly. "I understand."

Grinning in answer, Brad looked happily relieved. "That's great, Deena. I knew you would. You're really terrific."

That made me feel warm all over. I was glad I hadn't said something I would have regretted. As we drove out of the parking lot, however, I was silent. I turned to study Brad's profile, trying to see him as Tabitha might. He really was the best-looking boy I'd ever dated. His face was strong, with a well-defined nose that was straight and just right for the rest of his face. A muscle moved in his jaw whenever he talked. His hair was fairly short and always in place, except for one lock that would occasionally fall over his forehead. He would impatiently push it back into place. That really was his only mannerism. He was usually in complete control of himself.

All at once I had to look away out the window on my side of the car. A tiny pain clutched at my heart. I realized how alike Brad and Tabitha were. They were both tall and blond, both involved in school activities and very sure of themselves and their futures. I sighed to myself. What was it Patty had said at lunch, that I was becoming a Brad Matthews clone? I caught sight of myself in the window, the dark mass of hair, the heavy eyebrows scowling again. I was hardly that, I thought.

Did Tabitha realize all of this? Was that why she'd touched Brad's arm the way she had? Or had it been only an innocent action? Was I overreacting?

I glanced down at my hands folded in my lap. On the third finger of my left hand, I wore Brad's class ring. I rubbed my thumb across the lump of adhesive tape that I'd wrapped around the back to make it fit.

I was being dumb. I had no reason to be jealous, not so long as I was the one wearing his ring. If Tabitha meant to stir up anything between them with her new computer, it simply wouldn't work. And when Brad and I went on our picnic, everything would be positively wonderful and romantic.

By the time Brad had pulled into the driveway of my house, I was happy again and ready to talk. "What's a spread sheet?" I asked, thinking it was something Brad would like to discuss.

"Hmmm—what?" Brad said, turning off the ignition. I guess he'd been deep in his own thoughts. He glanced over at me then and smiled. "You really want to know?"

"Sure," I said. "Tell me. You know I'm interested in anything that interests you."

"Well," he said and leaned back, getting

comfortable, "a spread sheet is actually just a series of columns, something like in an account book. But with a spread-sheet software program, you can set up columns that have figures that interact with one another, such as in profit and loss statements. . . ."

And that's where he lost me. Or rather that was the point where I tuned out. But I kept the interested expression on my face as I began planning again what I was going to take on the picnic.

"That's really terrific," I said in a silent moment. "I can see why you're so excited about the idea of getting your own computer."

"Yeah," Brad agreed with a thoughtful nod of his head. "I live for the day."

"Uh-huh!" I smiled. "Brad, what kind of cheeses do you like?"

"Huh?" A puzzled look crossed his face.

"What kind of cheeses do you like?" I repeated. "You know, like swiss, or cheddar, or maybe brie? See, I was thinking of having french bread and some cheeses and fruit for our picnic instead of plain old sandwiches or fried chicken. Doesn't that sound good? What do you think?"

"Cheese—chicken?" The puzzled look was still there, but something else had been added, a slight frown. "Deena, just what are you talking about?"

"Our picnic, of course!" Now I felt myself beginning to frown. "What do you mean what am I talking about? I'm talking about this Saturday."

"But," Brad said, shaking his head, "I thought you said you understood?"

"I do!" I nodded. "I understand about your forgetting about Saturday for a minute, and I accept your apology."

"But Deena, I'm afraid you misunderstood me." Brad looked slightly unhappy. "I did apologize about forgetting about the picnic on Saturday. But that didn't mean I wasn't going to go to Tabitha's on Saturday instead. That's what I thought you understood." The puzzled look was back. "Now I don't understand! The way you talked just now, asking me about the spread sheets, I thought you were excited that I was going to get to use Tabitha's new computer."

"You mean you're really going to Tabitha's?" I asked.

"Well, yes!"

"Instead of our picnic?"

"Listen, Deena—" Brad said.

Angry thoughts were slithering into my mind. I was suddenly breathing hard. "I don't believe it!"

"Why can't we have a picnic the next Saturday?" he tried.

"Because—" My fingers wrapped themselves around Brad's ring. "Because—" Did I want to take it off, give it back to him? "Because—" I let go of the ring. I wasn't that angry. "Because," I said evenly, "next Saturday isn't the same. It *isn't* this Saturday!"

"But, Deena—" He sounded genuinely bewildered, but I didn't care.

"You don't understand, do you?" I yelled, pushing down hard on the door handle at the same time.

I knew I was shouting, but I couldn't stop. I jerked the car door open. "Well, just think about it, Brad." I stepped out of the car, then leaned down long enough to add, "I'll see you tomorrow, *maybe*!" I didn't want to see his eyes. I slammed the door shut and walked up our front walk without looking back. I opened the front door at the same time that I heard Brad's car start. Then I slammed that door, too.

And as the sound of his car died away, Mom poked her head out from the living room doorway. "Hi, Deena. How was your day?"

Chapter Two

The next morning I looked thoughtfully at Brad's ring, remembering the night he'd given it to me. For me it had been very romantic. And I had hoped that it would be only the beginning of many romantic moments, strung one after another.

But there hadn't been another romantic moment. And that's what I thought the picnic would be all about, a romantic day to remember and build on.

It wasn't as if I expected Brad to come roaring up with a bouquet of balloons the way Richard had. Brad was an entirely different sort of person.

Brad's maturity was one of the things I found most attractive about him. Whenever I was with him, I felt secure. He was exactly what I needed.

I liked to think I knew where my life was going; I knew I wanted to be a commercial artist. But, unlike Brad, I didn't have all the details planned out. That's why Brad was helping me pull my thoughts for my future together. Patty couldn't understand that and so she labeled Brad as boring and called me a Brad Matthews clone.

Brad had sat down with me and shown me that, along with my art classes, I really should take some business courses. Having them, he said, would be the basis for a *real* career. Like a lot of people, Brad's opinion of a career in art was that it was one big dream. He thought that once I was out of school I'd realize that. I'd never really argued the point with him. I'd tried with other people and just ended up feeling frustrated.

The business classes had seemed like a good idea. I even went to my counselor to see about signing up for them. If I dropped an art class from my schedule, I could take accounting and, possibly, typing instead.

But as I was waiting for the appointment with my counselor, I kept remembering what my art teacher, Mr. Lander, had told us. An art contest was being sponsored in our school by a few local advertising agencies, and the winner would spend the summer working in one of them as an intern, learning about the advertising business.

The very thought of winning was enough to keep me awake most of the night. The contest was open only to students taking commercial art. It was one of the classes I had planned to drop.

When the door to the counselor's office opened and the student who'd been inside left, I went in. I stood there for a second, then apologized. "I'm sorry," I said. "I've changed my mind. I don't want to change my schedule after all." I rushed out, afraid I would change my mind again.

Then I had to tell Brad. I told him I'd sign up for *summer* business classes instead. That way I could spend my time concentrating solely on them. The plan was logical, except for one tiny hitch. What if I won the art contest? How would I manage to juggle classes with a full-time internship at an agency? I told myself that summer was a few months off. I'd find a way somehow.

But right then I had another, more pressing problem. I had to make Brad realize that he'd made the wrong decision. That a day with Tabitha Wingford and her dumb computer in no way could compare with a wonderfully romantic day in the country with me.

                    *   *   *

By Friday I hadn't even made a dent in Brad's plan to spend Saturday with Tabitha. He drove me home after school. In front of my house, Brad put the car in park and turned off the ignition.

"Deena," Brad said, looking sincere and thoughtful, "I want you to know that I've been thinking about Saturday. Just the way you asked me to."

"Oh?" I held my breath.

"Yes." Brad nodded slowly. "I realize now how thoughtless it was of me to forget about the picnic you'd planned."

"Brad," I answered softly, feeling myself beginning to fall into the depths of his gray eyes. "It's all right. I understand."

Brad smiled. "I kind of thought you did. I've noticed how silent you've been the last couple of days, and I knew you must have felt stupid about having blown up the way you did Tuesday afternoon. But you don't have to apologize."

"Me?" I frowned. "Me, apologize?"

"Sure," Brad said. "I knew if I let you do some thinking on your own, you'd know how much more important it is for me to spend the day with Tabitha's computer than to go on the picnic. We can always do it some other day, right, Deena?"

Déjà vu time, I thought to myself. We'd had practically the same conversation Tuesday. I'd been stupid to think Brad would change his mind. "Why don't we just forget the whole thing," I said, getting out of the car. "Forget I ever mentioned the idea of a picnic. I'm certainly sorry I did."

"Deena." Brad reached over to grab my arm. "I don't get it. What's the problem?"

"Nothing." I shook his hand off. "There's absolutely no problem at all." I slipped out of the car, then leaned down into the window. "Have a great time tomorrow. And don't bother straining yourself thinking about me. I'll find some simple little activity to keep myself occupied." I slammed the door shut and, with my head held high, walked up the front walk and into the house.

I was about to go to my room where I could throw myself on the bed and stare at the ceiling and think evil thoughts about Tabitha. But at the bottom of the stairs, I halted. *I really will find something to do tomorrow*, I told myself. And it wasn't just going to be some simple little thing, the way I'd told Brad.

In the den, I searched through the papers on the desk until I found what I was looking for—the letter announcing I'd won the ten free flying lessons. I checked the phone number, picked up the phone, and dialed.

"Hello," I said. "Is this the Pinebrook Flying School?" I waited for the answer, then said, "This is Deena Whitney. I'd like to make an appointment for a lesson tomorrow morning."

Chapter Three

Pinebrook Airport is about six miles from the edge of town. It's a small airport, mainly used by private planes. I must have passed the dirt road leading to it hundreds of times while driving on the main highway to Danville and the shopping mall. But I hadn't known there was a flying school there until I'd received the letter telling me I'd won the lessons.

Now I was on my way there, driving Mom's car along the stretch of road at the bottom of the foothills. To my left was a scattering of pine and low brush; to my right, a slope of natural meadow, already bright with tiny purple and yellow wild flowers.

I felt a twist in my stomach. It was the meadow where I'd planned to have our picnic.

There was a picture-perfect little brook that ran through the center of it. I'd thought about putting down a blanket, then spreading out our lunch, perhaps picking some of the flowers for a centerpiece. It would have been a scene straight out of a love story. But, no, Brad had preferred to be inside, cooped up in a stuffy room with a computer and—

I shook my head, refusing to think about who would be cooped up with Brad.

Soon the pine trees and the meadow were behind me. Stretching out on either side of the road were farms. White fences blurred as I drove past. In one pasture black and white cows munched their way across patches of new grass. On the other side freshly turned earth lay rich and dark in long furrows. I could see the tractor in the distance that had made them. Rolling down the car window, I inhaled deeply. I loved the smell of damp earth.

What would those fields look like from up in the air? I wondered. I could remember seeing photos of fields plowed into patterns; photos taken from a plane. Now I would have a chance to see for myself. Soon!

Oh, my gosh, I thought as adrenaline raced through my veins. What was I doing? This might be my last hour alive on this planet. If I were smart, I'd turn the car around and head for home. My palms became sweaty as I envisioned myself in a tiny plane, thousands of feet up in the air, with nothing between the earth and my body but the thin, metal shell of a plane. What if the engine should fail? The plane would go zooming down, down, down to the ground. We'd crash and go up in flames.

I pictured Brad, tearful because he knew my death was his fault. I could see him standing beside my open grave, distraught, finally throwing himself across the coffin that held my poor broken body. The trouble was that I could see Tabitha there as well. She was standing next to Brad. Then they'd walk away together. And I'd be left there, in a hole in the ground. Yes, I should definitely have turned around and gone home. But I didn't.

The man who had answered the phone on Friday afternoon had sounded very competent. His voice had been mature, kind of middle-aged. I'd pictured him with graying hair and gentle eyes. Someone like that would certainly have spent a great deal of time in a plane. And he was alive. I was being ridiculously chicken.

But when I pulled into the parking lot beside a long, rusty metal building, I was still more than mildly nervous. I sat still and took several deep breaths, which made me feel a little better.

I got out of the car and locked it. There were several other cars near mine, yet I didn't see anyone walking around. For an airport, it seemed terribly deserted. There was a chain link fence dividing the parking area from the airport itself. A row of small planes was lined up on the other side of the fence. Was one of those the one I would be flying? There was one solid blue one, and the rest were white with either red or blue markings.

I walked around the end of the metal building, looking for a door. But there was only a gate with an arrow pointing toward a second building. A faded sign above the arrow read "Pinebrook Flying School." I followed the arrow, hoping their airplanes were in better shape than the sign.

The school office wasn't in the second building either. There was only another arrow. Frustrated, I went on to the third building. Finally, on the far side, I found the office. A wooden screen door hung not quite flush with the frame. I pulled it open and entered a dim room.

As my eyes began to adjust to the darkness, I saw a long counter dividing the room. Standing in front of it were two people, a middle-aged man, very much like the one I'd pictured in my mind, and someone much younger. My entrance had apparently interrupted a conversation between them. I thought about apologizing and suggesting I come back later when the older man smiled and asked, "Would you be Deena Whitney?"

"Yes," I said, nodding. "Mr. Gillian?"

"Right," he answered, checking the watch on his wrist. "You're just a few minutes early. If you'll have a seat over there on that couch," he said, pointing to a piece of ancient leather furniture, "I'll be with you in a second." He didn't bother introducing me to the person standing next to him.

As I sat, air sighed out through several cracks in the couch, pushing white bits of stuffing out with it. Once settled, I pretended to examine what looked like photographs on the far wall. But as my eyes grew accustomed to the dim light of the room, I realized what I was pretending to look at with such interest weren't photos at all, but pieces of paper stuck there. And because it seemed dumb to be staring at something like that, I pretended to examine the rest of the room. I stopped pretending, though, as soon as I realized that no one was paying any attention to me. From the tone of their voices, they seemed to be having an argument.

The other person had shifted his position, and I could now see his face. I was kind of surprised. Earlier, because of the greasy over-alls he was wearing, I'd thought he was a mechanic. But now I could see he was about my own age. Someone my age wouldn't be given the responsibility of keeping planes fit to fly.

Maybe he was a part-time janitor. I tried to decide if he was good-looking. It was hard to tell from the way he was frowning. His hair was dark brown, wavy, and thick. His skin was dark, too, a deep bronze, as if he spent a lot of time working out in the open. I thought his mouth might be nice, if he didn't look so grim. And his eyes, they looked—black.

Suddenly I realized that those black eyes were staring straight at me, practically drill-ing through me. They accused me of being rude for staring the way I was. Embarrassed at being caught, I dropped my gaze as a hot flush creeped up my neck.

I wanted to get up, to run out of the room, to drop through the floor, anything but stay where I was. But I didn't. And after a few minutes of silence I realized there were no longer three of us in the room. There were only two. Mr. Gillian was standing alone by the counter. As I looked up, he smiled at me, then picked up a clipboard from the top of the counter and started toward me.

"Sorry about that," he apologized in a friendly but gruff manner. "Seems there's always something that needs handling." Giving me the clipboard and a ballpoint pen, he added, "Here are a couple of forms you'll need to fill out before you can fly. You can get busy on them while I go check out which plane is available for us to use."

I watched him as he disappeared through the door, leaving it bouncing slightly on its hinges. As I bent over the forms, I wondered if the argument had been moved outside, away from my ears.

I concentrated on filling in the blank spaces. Whatever was going on was none of my business, as the black eyes had strongly warned me. All at once my hand froze, the pen poised above a word. "Death." I was to fill in the name of someone who could be notified in case of my accidental death.

What was I doing filling out a form like this? Terror surged through me. This piece of paper was hinting strongly that I just might die. I didn't want anyone notified. I didn't want anyone to have to be notified. Something had to be all wrong here. Mr. Gillian had been upset and had handed me the wrong form. Sure, that was it. I would wait until he came back and ask for the right one. I laid the clipboard down on the couch and stood up. I felt calm. It was just a mistake.

For something to do, I walked across the room. I would go see what those pieces of paper were that I'd noticed earlier. But as I stood in front of them I realized they weren't pieces of paper. They were shirttails. Shirttails that had been carefully cut from complete shirts, then pinned to the wall. Shirttails cut from whose shirts? Accident victims? Others who had filled out forms in this very office? Hung there like so many scalps?

Then I saw that each piece of shirt had something printed on it in felt-tip ink. I leaned closer to the one in front of me. There was the name of a person, a date, and what had to be the identification number of a plane. I read, "Rick Gillian, Cessna 151, N714QQ." The date was a little over four years ago. Had Rick been a relative of Mr. Gillian's? If so, how could he possibly keep such a reminder on the wall of his office?

Suddenly I was aware of a voice coming through a half-open window close by. I recognized it as Mr. Gillian's and decided it must be the continuation of the argument, as I'd suspected. But then I heard the second voice. It was a woman's, and she was hysterical.

"I tell you, I am not going to go up again with that person. I mean it!" The voice rose nearly two octaves. "We came close to crashing. I know it. As surely as I'm standing here talking to you. And all I could think of was that we had no parachutes." Mr. Gillian tried to break into the conversation, but she cut him off. "Don't waste your breath. There isn't a thing you could say that would change my mind. The power went dead, and the next thing I knew we were hurtling toward the ground. . . ."

That was all I needed to hear. What with the "scalps" hanging on the wall and this woman describing her near death, I no longer wanted to take lessons. I felt just the way she did. There was no way I was going to go up in some death trap.

Grabbing my purse from where I'd left it on the couch, I bolted for the door. There I paused. The problem was getting past Mr. Gillian without having to go into a long explanation as to why I was suddenly leaving. And in order to get back to my car, the way I'd reached the office, I would have to go past him. He was standing in the middle of the path.

I would just have to find another way, perhaps by going behind this building. Quietly I slipped through the screen door and moved stealthily to the corner to check for an opening.

I made it out. But three buildings and five

turns later I was hopelessly confused. Then I saw what I thought might be the parking lot, straight ahead, between two rickety sheds. I strode purposefully in that direction. I was in an open area. It wasn't the parking lot, but at least I wasn't lost among the buildings. All I had to do now was keep walking in the right direction, and sooner or later I'd reach my car. I hoped it would be sooner, before Mr. Gillian missed me and came looking for me.

I guess I was so preoccupied with the idea of finding my car that I didn't see the blur of blue approaching from my left until it was too late. And then I was flying through the air. I'd been hit. The next thing I knew I was lying face down, staring at black asphalt, both my knees and one elbow hurting like crazy, and something heavy crushing me.

"Are you completely insane?" a familiar male voice yelled directly into my right ear.

"Huh?" I sputtered into the asphalt. By turning my head a little, I saw a grease-covered hand about three inches away from my nose. "Just what do you think you're doing?" I asked in as hostile a voice as I could manage with no air in my lungs.

"Saving your life," the voice replied. Then all at once the weight was gone from my back, and I was being lifted to my feet. "There," he said, turning me. "Do you see that plane?" I nodded. A blue plane was moving along the asphalt, about fifty feet away from where we were standing.

"So?" I asked.

"So, you just about had your head knocked off by the wing on that plane." The hands still holding my shoulders turned me again. I was now looking into the same black, unfriendly eyes I'd looked into in Mr. Gillian's office. If anything they were even less friendly. "Don't you know any better than to walk down the middle of a taxi strip?"

"Taxi strip?"

"Yes. Taxi strip." He took his hands off my shoulders to gesture angrily toward a yellow line down the center of the asphalt. "What are you doing in this area anyway? Can't you read? There are signs posted all over that say, 'No students are allowed in this area without an instructor.' "

I hadn't seen any signs. But I hadn't exactly come by the usual route. I was feeling like an idiot. *He* was making me feel like an idiot. I was also shaken to the core. Planes weren't even safe on the ground. I stuck my chin out. "I'm not a student. So the signs don't apply to me."

"But—" The black eyes narrowed, and he tipped his head to one side as if trying to figure out something. "Back in the office Frank told me you *were* a student."

"Well, he was wrong," I snapped. "What's more," I said, sweeping an arm around at the buildings, "I wouldn't be a student at this crummy airport if you paid me. The place is practically falling down. I hate to think what the planes must be like." I could see a flush of anger wash across his face as I said that. But I went right on. "Now, if you'll kindly show me the way out of here, I'll be more than delighted to get off your stupid taxi strip."

"The exit," he said through clenched teeth, "is right through that gate." And as he said it, he jerked a thumb in the direction of a gate that would have leaped out and bit me if it had been alive. To top it off there was a sign above it with Parking Lot printed in bold letters.

"Oh," I said with a flip of my head. "Thank you." Then, with great dignity, I walked toward the gate.

"You know," he called after me, "it's a good thing you aren't a student. You probably couldn't find your way to the take-off area. And if you did, you'd probably take off in the wrong direction and kill someone."

I whirled around. "Oh, really!"

"Yes!" he added. "It's not hard to see you don't have the stuff it takes to be a pilot."

"Oh, really!" I repeated idiotically. "Is that so?" But he wasn't going to let me have the final word. He'd already turned and was walking away.

Chapter Four

Mom was in the kitchen, ironing board set up, working on a pile of about three weeks' laundry. My dad travels a lot and always brings home a load of dirty shirts. She glanced up as I came through the back door.

"So," she asked, smiling, "is it Pilot Deena now?"

"Afraid not," I answered glumly. Hoisting myself onto a stool, I reached for an apple from the bowl on the counter. "I blew it." I lifted the apple to my mouth and bit into it, almost viciously.

"Um-hmmm." Mom raised an eyebrow. "And do you feel like telling me what happened?"

I set the apple down on the counter.

"Mom," I said, looking at her, "I don't believe what I did. I chickened out."

"I see." She nodded. "Well, I guess I can understand how you're feeling right now. If it had been me, I would consider chickening out a wise move." She smiled as she pulled an ironed shirt off the board. "But *you*," she said, picking another shirt out of the pile, and pulling it onto the board, "I'm a bit surprised. I've spent my entire life, since you were born, wondering what you were going to try next. I honestly thought you'd come racing home to announce you'd decided to give up the world of art for the world of commercial flying."

"Mom!"

"Oh, all right," she said. "So I exaggerated just a little. But I really am interested in hearing about what happened." She paused for a moment, looking thoughtful. "And what are you going to do with the rest of your prize if you don't want to take any more lessons?"

"Mom, listen to me." I waved my hands to get her to realize how serious I was. "You wouldn't want me to go there again. You've got to see this place to believe it. I know the airport isn't safe. All the buildings look like they're about to fall down. And, well, there was this woman, she was talking about crashing. Or at least almost crashing. She was a student. And, if she almost crashed, well . . ." I ran out of words.

"You're kidding! That does sound a little scary. Tell me, did the woman tell you this directly?"

"Uh, no." I shook my head. What did that matter? "I overheard her talking to the man who runs the flying school. She was complaining about one of the instructors."

"And," Mom asked looking over at me, holding the iron poised above the shirt, "just how did the man answer her?"

"I—I guess I didn't wait to hear," I admitted.

Mom set the iron down on its heel. "You mean you left without hearing what he had to say?" She sounded surprised.

"Yes," I answered. "But—"

"Deena, I can't believe what I'm hearing." Mom sounded almost angry. "The woman could have simply been some hysterical creature who never should have tried flying in the first place. How do you know that the plane didn't just hit an air pocket or something, and she frightened herself into believing the plane was about to crash?"

"Oh!" Chagrined, I looked at Mom.

"Right." Mom looked back at me wryly. "Seems you got a bit hysterical yourself." She tipped her head to one side. "So, are you going to go back and take a lesson?"

"I can't." I closed my eyes, remembering how I'd run out. "I left without telling the instructor I was going. Now I'm too embarrassed to go back." But it wasn't Mr. Gillian I was seeing in my mind's eye. It was the boy with the black eyes. I never, ever, wanted to have to come face to face with him again. And if I went back, there was every possibility I would run in to him. After all, the airport wasn't very big.

"Oh, Deena, how could you?" Mom's disapproving voice made me open my eyes. "That was just plain bad manners. Not to mention the fact that you made an appointment, then didn't keep it. Don't you realize you cost the flying school money by doing that?"

"I'm sorry," I said, slumping over.

"I'm not the one to whom you should be apologizing." Her look was stern. "Quite frankly, I think you should go into the den this minute, pick up the phone, call that man, and apologize. Maybe you can offer to pay for the lesson you didn't take."

"It was a free lesson," I argued.

"Not for someone," she said right back.

"I don't know why you're getting this way with me," I argued. "I didn't want to win the

42

stupid lessons in the first place. And I *have* paid for them. I bought the raffle tickets. But what I wanted was the second prize, the typewriter."

"Deena." Mom had started ironing again. "If you wanted the typewriter in the first place, why did you go ahead and make an appointment for a lesson? Why didn't you see if you could exchange the lessons for the typewriter? The lessons are certainly worth more. I'm sure whoever won the typewriter would have been willing to trade."

"That's exactly what I was going to do," I answered lamely. "Then I guess—well, I guess I thought it might be fun to try flying after all." I looked down at my hands. I hadn't told Mom about my fight with Brad. I didn't want to talk to my mother about the problems I was having with him. I'd made an excuse about our canceling the picnic by saying that Brad had something terribly important to do that day.

"And after making the appointment and getting all the way out to the airport, you decided it wouldn't be so much fun after all. Right?"

"Mom, I told you—" I gave up in midsentence. Mom had just proved to me what a really dumb move I'd made. I slipped off the stool. "I guess I'll go into the den and make that call."

43

Mr. Gillian was very nice on the phone. I was sure he had guessed why I'd left, but he didn't say anything to make me feel like I wanted to crawl into a hole. He said he'd be happy to reschedule another appointment when I'd made up my mind about whether or not I wanted the lessons. There was no time limit on them.

After hanging up the phone, I sat there for a moment. The letter was still on the top of the desk. The names of the second and third prize winners were listed in the letter, right under my name. I could call the guy with the type-writer right now. I reached for the phone again. But I stopped, my hand on the receiver. I didn't really feel like talking to anyone else at the moment. I'd call later in the afternoon. *Yes*, I thought, nodding to myself. *I'll do that.*

I left the den and went upstairs to my room. I changed out of the clothes I was wear-ing into my "at home" clothes, an ancient sweat shirt and really ancient jeans. I decided to spend the afternoon working on a project for Mr. Lander's design class. It was due first thing Monday morning. I would at least get something accomplished that day, I told myself. I would *not* waste an afternoon moping around, thinking of Brad and Tabitha.

I couldn't concentrate. Sitting down at my

worktable, I got as far as pulling my sketch-book toward me to do the preliminary sketches. I stared at the blank paper. The project was to be a three-dimensional, abstract design in paper and wire. It was to be, in Mr. Lander's words, "A depiction of your own perception of your current environment." If I put all the feelings aroused by *my* current environment into a three-dimensional figure, Mr. Lander would be sure to send me straight off to the school psychiatrist. Or flunk me.

I pushed the pad away from me, then got up, and walked over to my window. I stared out at the still beautiful day and at the cloudless sky. A few minutes later I decided what I would do. I went back to my worktable, sat down, and picked up my pencil.

On Monday morning Brad pulled his car into the drive and honked. I carefully carried the finished project out to the car. Seeing my hands were full, Brad leaped from the driver's side and came around to open the door for me. Then as he saw what I was carrying up close, he paused. I could practically see the wheels going around in his head as he wondered whether to compliment me or just break down and ask what the thing was. Brad's practical side won out.

"I don't want to upset you, Deena," he

said. "But would you mind telling me what *that* is?"

"It's a class project," I answered sweetly, sliding into my side of the front seat. I reached out and pulled the door shut. I didn't exactly slam it in his face, but I was on the verge of it.

I could see him glance at me through the windshield as he walked around the front of the car to get back in the driver's seat. We drove two blocks before he spoke again. "Well, it's very nice," he said. "Whatever it's supposed to be."

"It's not supposed to be nice," I said, and then I shut up. I suppose it was crummy of me, but I was enjoying his uneasiness. It was so rare to see Brad unsure of himself or of what to say.

"OK, then it's beautiful."

"No." I looked down at my project. "I certainly would never call it beautiful."

We drove three more blocks, all in total silence. I reached down and casually adjusted a piece of wire.

"What class is it for?" Brad asked finally.

"Design," I replied. He was still guessing. I wasn't about to give him any real clues.

"Ah-ha!" He looked smug. "Now I get it. It isn't supposed to be anything. It's an—an abstract. Right?"

"Close," I said.

We pulled into the student parking lot. Brad eased the car into an extrawide parking space, giving himself plenty of room on either side. He hated it when people banged their car doors open into his car and put scratches in the paint.

Brad shut off the engine, then paused, his hand still on the keys hanging in the ignition. "So," he asked, sounding casual, "what did you do on Saturday?"

For a second I sat there, feeling as if I'd momentarily stuck my finger into an electrical outlet. Had Brad found out about the flying lessons? Before I had a chance to explain? Then I really looked at him. The way he looked wasn't angry, it was—almost guilty. Why?

"I worked on this," I said, replying to his question. I felt a little guilty myself. But I wasn't exactly lying, just doing a little editing. "It's called *Decisions*. See," I added, "this little figure up here, hanging onto this wire and about to fall, is supposed to represent me. And this black cube down here is supposed to represent—"

"Deena, listen!" Brad cut me off before I could tell him he was the black cube. Brad turned in his seat, putting his arm along the back. He absently tugged at a loose thread in the upholstery. "I thought about what *I* did on Saturday, how I went to Tabitha's to use the

47

computer. I realize now that you had every right to be angry. I was being selfish, just thinking how excited I was about getting the chance to use the computer. And I want you to know that I'm really sorry." To prove he meant what he said, he moved his hand, gently encircling my shoulders with his arm. "Really sorry."

"Oh!" I answered back softly, clutching *Decisions* and almost dislodging the black cube.

"Watch it," Brad cautioned. "You don't want to ruin whatever that's supposed to represent before you get it to class."

"No, absolutely," I answered with a secret smile. "I wouldn't want to do that."

"So, Deena," he said softly, "am I forgiven?"

Looking into those gray eyes, my heart thudded in my chest. How could I possibly say anything other than yes? Our lips were only inches apart. "You know you are."

Then Brad's lips met mine in the sweetest of kisses.

Chapter Five

With Brad's kiss fresh in my mind, I went to my counselor's office before school began. I had decided that, if Brad was bending in my direction, the least I could do would be to go ahead and sign up for those summer business courses. And I promised myself I would definitely take them, no matter what. I wouldn't even *think* art this summer. I would be the kind of girlfriend who was worthy of a boy like Brad.

The only problem was that sign-ups for summer classes wouldn't begin for another week. I left the office disappointed. I'd really wanted to tell Brad, that afternoon, that I'd signed up. Now I'd have to wait an entire week to surprise him.

Mr. Lander had to pick that very day to fill

us in on the details of the ad agency contest. I thought about what would happen if I managed to win the internship and was signed up for summer business courses as well. Would I be able to handle both? I'd have to. I was going to take the business classes because I loved Brad and trusted him to know what was best for my future. But the contest was also about my future. Winning would give me a real boost into the world of advertising—a world I definitely wanted to be a part of.

Yet when I went to work on the first sketches for the make-believe ad campaign, my drawings were dreadful. It wasn't like any work I'd done before. It wasn't me at all. And I couldn't understand what was happening.

Those preliminary sketches for three print ads were to be handed in to Mr. Lander on Friday morning. On Friday there was nothing to do but turn them in.

"Deena," he said at the end of class, "I'd like you to stay for a few minutes." Then after the other students had left the room, he propped my work up against the board. "What's happening here? Where's your usual style?"

"It's not there?" I asked, trying to make it sound as if I didn't know what he was talking about. But I did agree with him.

"No, it's definitely not." He gestured

toward my work. "This is so tight. Just look at it! Everything is small and pushed to the center, as if you're afraid to reach out to the edge of the paper." He looked at me. "Where's that free-flowing Deena Whitney style?"

I stared at my work, not saying anything. It was true, I was cowering there in the center of the page, keeping a protective border of white around me.

"I'd like to give this back to you, Deena," he said. Gathering up the sheets of paper, he put them into my portfolio and handed it to me. "Give the assignment another try this weekend. Bring in something new Monday morning. All right?"

For the rest of the day I felt really low. Maybe it was naive of me to want an art career. If I couldn't be consistent in my work, how could I ever expect to make a living with it? But the longer I thought about it, the more certain I was that there wasn't anything else I really wanted to do with my life. I wanted to be a commercial artist. It didn't matter that I was currently in a slump because it was only a matter of time before I was good again.

I was still in a low mood when Brad drove me home. And when he suggested we go to a movie, I pleaded a headache. I just wanted to stay home and think about why I hadn't been capable of turning out decent work.

Pouring myself a glass of milk, I carried it into the den, then flipped on the TV set and tuned in to MTV. Sometimes, if I watched the music videos my creative juices would start flowing.

But my creativity didn't have a chance because, oddly enough, the only thing I could see was the scene from Saturday at the airport played out in brilliant colors. I'd acted like a coward, and didn't my drawings reflect that? Frightened, cowardly images huddled into the center of the page? What was I afraid of? If I faced up to that, would my art be OK again?

There was only one way to find out. I picked up the phone and dialed. If I could manage to get a lesson for the morning, I would still have all weekend to work on the drawings.

I pulled the car into the parking lot at the airport, and I had to admit that the buildings weren't so old and beat up as I'd told my mother they were. Sure, they all could use a new coat of paint, but they weren't going to collapse. The grounds were neat and free of trash. The path leading to the school office had fresh gravel on it.

Mr. Gillian was waiting for me in the office. His smile made me feel instantly at ease, as if I were an old friend and not a new student.

After I filled out the papers, which weren't all that terrible after all, he surprised me by saying there'd be a change. It turned out he wasn't going to be my instructor.

"But," he said as he winked, "I think you won't mind. It's my nephew who'll be giving you your lesson today. He's a lot closer to your age. In fact, he's a high-school senior. Over in Danville."

How could I tell him I didn't want someone even remotely close to my own age teaching me to fly? I wanted someone old enough to know what he was doing. "Yep," Mr. Gillian said, giving my shoulder a friendly slap. "You and Rick'll get along just swell. I know it. I taught him everything he knows about flying. And he's a mighty good instructor, everyone says so, even though he's only had his license for three months."

"Three months?" I managed to whisper.

"Well, yeah," Mr. Gillian kind of drawled. " 'Course he's been flying a plane since he was about that height." Mr. Gillian put his hand out in the air, somewhere about knee level. "Rick Gillian's a name that'll go down in the history of flying."

"Rick—Rick Gillian?" Somehow the name sounded familiar. Where had I heard it? Or seen it? Then it sank in. I'd seen his name on one of those cut-off shirttails hanging on the wall, one of those grisly mementos from a plane crash. "But—but," I said, pointing to the wall, "he's dead!"

"What?" Mr. Gillian's bushy gray eyebrows shot straight up. "What on God's green earth made you think such a fool thing?"

Stammering, I began to explain. I'd only gotten as far as the part about my thinking that the shirttails were some sort of modern-day scalps when I noticed Mr. Gillian was close to falling over with silent laughter.

"Oh, Deena, Deena," he said, catching his breath and wiping away some tears sliding down his cheeks. "You do have quite an imagination." He started laughing again, then stopped himself. "I can see why you scooted out of here in such a hurry last week. Young lady," he said, "let me tell you about a sacred tradition."

Then he explained how the shirttails were a source of pride for their former owners. After a person goes on his first flight alone, called a solo, the tail of his or her shirt is cut off by the instructor. The person's name, as well as the identification number of the plane and the date, is printed on the shirttail in ink. Finally the tail is pinned to the wall of the flying school office for everyone to see.

Minutes later, still feeling numb about what an idiot I'd made of myself, I followed Mr. Gillian out to the hangar to meet his nephew.

As we drew closer to where the planes were parked, however, the numbness began to wear off, and a quiet excitement took its place. The plane we walked toward was white with red trim. It shone prettily in the sun.

Mr. Gillian noticed the approval registered on my face. "Yep," he said and smiled. "She is a pretty little thing, isn't she? And she handles real nice. Just the way a plane should with a lady at the controls."

"What kind is it?" I asked.

"A Cessna One fifty." Then he pointed to a number on the side of the plane. "See that?"

I nodded, figuring it must be something like the license plate on a car.

"That's the identification number. Each time you fly, you come into the office and log the number of the plane you flew and how long you flew. In this case it would be N-seven-one-four-Q-Q. And that's how you keep track of the hours you have in the air. It's very important. You have to have so many instructor hours and so many solo hours officially logged in before you can get your private pilot's license."

"I see," I said. I didn't want to explain that there would be only one hour logged in my book, that I only intended to take just this one lesson.

"Also, whenever you refer to this particular plane on the radio, you'll say, 'This is N-Seven-One-Four-Quebec-Quebec. Understand?" I smiled. "But officially her name is *Quack-Quack*." He chuckled. "You like that?"

Suddenly I found Mr. Gillian's warmth and humor overtaking me, and I was laughing with him. "Yes," I answered. "I think I like the idea of flying in a plane named *Quack-Quack*."

I was still smiling as we reached the side of the plane. Rick Gillian was there already.

My smile disappeared. "You!"

The black eyes narrowed. "I don't believe it!"

Mr. Gillian gave a little grunt. "Well, well. You two seem to know each other already."

I stayed silent.

Rick said, "We've met," in a cold, formal voice.

Mr. Gillian shot a look back and forth between us. "Do I detect a problem?"

"Well—" I said.

"No, sir," Rick said.

Mr. Gillian looked at me.

"No—huh-uh," I managed to get out.

"Good!" He scrutinized both Rick and me. Then he patted me on the shoulder, while giving Rick a serious look. "The inside of a cockpit is much too small a space for animosity."

"Yes, sir," Rick repeated.

Mr. Gillian nodded, then I received one more fatherly pat before he turned to walk away.

Rick said in a completely impersonal tone, "The first thing anyone does before taking a plane up is to do what we call a preflight check. It's a safety precaution that should never, never be neglected." He paused, regarding me as if I were someone he'd never exchanged words with before. "Is that clear?"

"Yes," I answered. "That's perfectly clear." I let my reply have a slight edge to it, to let him know I still remembered his taunts from the week before.

"Very good," Rick answered evenly. "Then if you'll follow me as I walk completely around the plane, I'll show you exactly what we do to make certain the plane is ready to fly." Rick began to move down one side of the plane toward the tail. I followed. As he went, he unhooked the line holding the plane's wing to the ground on that side. But as he began to explain about checking the fuel tanks and the control wires, I did the same thing I did when Brad talked about spread sheets. I only half listened. There was no real reason to pay attention. I wouldn't be doing this again.

Instead, I spent the time walking around the plane behind Rick studying him. My impression of him that day was almost totally different from the first Saturday.

Now he was dressed in pressed gray cords and a forest green turtleneck jersey that turned his already tan complexion even more bronze. The lightweight gray jacket he wore over it outlined his shoulders. The previous Saturday I'd thought he was thin. He wasn't. It was just that he wasn't overly muscular. Yet the way his cords fit over his hips and thighs showed he was a person with strength.

If I weren't so much in love with Brad Matthews, I thought, I could find Rick Gillian intriguing—if, of course, he didn't have such an irritating personality. I'd just convinced myself of that when he turned to face me, catching me totally off guard with a question.

"Did you get all of that?" he asked, thrusting what looked like an oil dipstick from a car in my face.

"Ah—uh—yes," I stammered, backing away from the oily thing.

"And did everything we checked look right to you?"

"Uh—" I paused. Was this some kind of trick question? Was I supposed to notice something wrong? Biting briefly at my lower lip, I took a chance and guessed. "Everything

58

looked fine to me." My brain clicked, and I added, "But I'm not the authority, am I?"

"Right. On both counts," Rick replied in a stern voice. But then he did something I hadn't seen him do before. He smiled. I knew he'd have a nice smile. It was wide and generous, and his teeth flashed white against the deep tan of his face.

I couldn't help myself; I found that I was smiling back.

Rick reached up and affectionately patted the side of the plane. "So the next thing on the list is to go flying."

Chapter Six

Rick showed me the tiny step on the side of the plane from which I could hoist myself into the cockpit. He showed me where my seat belt was, then shut the door. While he walked around the front of the plane to get in on the other side, I realized the tremendous difference between admiring a plane from the outside and being inside one.

When you're outside, the entire world is out there with you. When you're inside, shut off from all outside noises, with limited visibility through rather small windows, crammed into a space that makes the interior of a VW Bug seem immense by comparison, the word claustrophobia takes on a brand-new meaning.

I glanced at the bank of instruments and

knobs lined up directly in front of me. Did a person actually have to learn to read all of those in order to fly this tiny plane? It was a good thing that I was only going to take one lesson. I knew I'd never be able to distinguish one of those dials from another. I'm just not a technically minded person.

"I'm sorry, did you say something?" Rick had swung himself into the seat beside me without my realizing it.

"Huh—what?" I asked.

"I thought you were saying something as I climbed in," Rick replied, swiveling back so that our eyes were now about six inches apart. He wasn't even leaning toward me. It was definitely a cozy area. I could almost feel the heat from his leg on mine.

"Did I?" I asked, laughing. It sounded weak. "Maybe I was talking out loud to myself." I tried to make a joke. "You know what they say, when you talk to yourself you're in good company."

"I guess I never heard that saying," Rick replied. "Well, someone else said that you learn something new every day." He smiled an instructorlike smile. "But now suppose you concentrate on learning something about flying. All right?"

"Yes," I said, catching myself before I added "sir."

Rick reached over to my side, unhooked a little wire gizmo from the wheel, did something with a couple of knobs at the bottom of what I was mentally calling the dashboard, and reached across my knee to where the key hung in the ignition. He didn't turn the key immediately. His hand just stayed there, lightly resting on my knee.

"When I start the engine, you'll find it slightly noisy. So I'm going to explain what I'll do from this point until we get up in the air. Then we'll go from there," Rick finished.

I nodded, very conscious of his hand. He continued.

"First of all, you're probably wondering why I'm sitting over here on this side, when all the controls seem to be situated on your side. That's because you're sitting on the pilot's side, the command side. And I want you over there, so you'll get used to it. Think of it as learning to drive a car."

I tried, but I couldn't seem to make the connection. Cars stayed on the ground. We were going up.

"Now, I presume that you understand the reason for that yellow line out there," Rick said meaningfully.

"Oh, you mean the taxi strip?" I asked with what I hoped sounded like sweet innocence.

But Rick didn't bite. He simply went on with his little prepared speech. "We'll taxi down it until we reach what is called the 'run up area.' That's an area at the end of the runway where we stop the plane and do another check list." I stared, wondering how long it was going to take to get one tiny plane up in the air. "One of the reasons is to make sure the engine's working properly. I'll push the throttle to full power while keeping my feet on the brakes. The proper term for what I will do is 'run up the engine,' thus the name of the area. Then if everything's OK, I'll turn the plane in a tight circle as I visually look in all directions to check the sky for possible planes in the area. If there are none, that's when we take off."

"Sounds simple enough," I said, trying to appear cool.

"I'm glad you think so," Rick replied and finally turned the key.

The engine roared to life, sounding as if four or five mountain lions had taken up residence just on the other side of the dashboard-instrument panel. Rick pulled on one of the knobs, and the plane began to move slowly forward.

Suddenly nervous, I tried to swallow but discovered my mouth had gone dry in the short time since Rick had turned the key. This was it. There was no backing out now. I was actually going through with this stupid, dumb, ridiculous idea.

I gripped the edge of my seat and closed my eyes. Why had I ever bought those raffle tickets in the first place? Just then I noticed that the plane had stopped going forward. It was standing still. Not only that, the engine didn't seem to be as loud. I opened my eyes to see what had happened and found Rick staring at me.

"Is something wrong?" I said.

"Are you really sure you want to take a lesson?" Rick inquired.

"Yes, of course," I replied. "Why?"

"Because most people wait until they're up in the air to become white-knuckle fliers. You're doing it while we're still on the taxi strip."

"Oh, that." I looked down at my hands. I made myself unclench them. "I do that all the time. It doesn't mean a thing."

Rick gave me this weird stare but then said, "OK. If you say so." Then he went back to looking straight ahead, gave the plane some gas, and we bounced on down the taxi strip. When we came to the run up area, he did exactly what he'd told me he was going to do. I was fine until he got to the point where he gave the engine full power. The mountain lion noise in front of us increased, as if the four original lions had invited ten more. As Rick held his feet on the brakes, the plane rattled and roared, sounding ready to launch itself into the air and self-destruct. I couldn't help it, I grabbed for the sides of my seat again, not caring if Rick saw me.

Rick didn't notice. He was too busy with the plane, all business. I could feel myself holding my breath as I watched what he was doing. He pulled back on one knob, and the plane's engine dropped to a semiroar. He took his foot off the brake on one side, and the plane turned in a tight circle as he scanned the sky above us. All too soon we were racing down the runway, faster and faster and faster, until the asphalt beneath us blurred and then dropped away. There was a sudden decrease of the sounds that had been the plane rattling as we'd raced over the ground. The nose seemed to go straight up as we passed over the tops of the trees that marked the end of the runway.

We were flying!

I was still gripping the edges of my seat, but I was also grinning. It was a strange sensation. I was terrified, yet I was thrilled. I wanted to yell to everyone below that this was absolutely the best feeling ever.

Rick turned the plane, and we continued to climb. "We're still within the landing pattern," he explained over the engine. "When we get out of it, we can turn anyway we want, but within the pattern, the pilot must maintain the flow."

The windshield was now filled, top to bottom, with blue sky. The mountain lions had quieted down and were now gently purring. I let go of the sides of the seat and put my hands in my lap.

"We'll fly out to what's called the practice area." Rick glanced over at me briefly. "That simply means it's an unpopulated spot where, if you crash, the only person you're likely to kill is yourself."

"Oh, terrific!" I responded nervously. But I managed to keep my hands in my lap.

"Don't worry." Rick smiled. "No one's been killed out there yet." He glanced down at my hands, tightly clenched into fists. "We'll take it easy. I won't push anything on you that you're not ready for."

By the time my lesson was almost over, I knew that I loved flying.

"Once more?" I asked eagerly. "I want to make just one more turn before we have to go back."

"OK." Rick's voice was easy. "But only one more. Then we really have to head back."

Carefully I pushed on the left rudder

pedal, turning the wheel at the same time. The plane responded, swinging in a wide circle before I straightened it out again. "Oh, Rick, I love flying." I felt like hugging myself, like hugging Rick because I was so excited. But I couldn't. I was too busy *flying*. "I've never felt this way before. I can't even begin to explain how I feel."

Rick was silent for a moment, then he said, "I know, Deena. I know exactly what you mean." He reached over to take the controls again.

As I relinquished them, I glanced over at Rick. The look on his face told me he did know exactly how I felt because he'd been there too.

"It doesn't seem as if it's been an hour," I said. "It seems more like half an hour."

"Actually," Rick said, grinning broadly, "It's been an hour and a half."

"You're kidding?" I stared. "But—well, will you get in trouble for being overtime?"

"I don't think so," Rick replied. "But if I do, it was worth it." There was a hint of a smile in his voice.

"Why?" I asked.

"Because"—Rick's eyes were warm as they met mine—"it's my way of saying I'm sorry for the way I acted last Saturday."

"I'd like to apologize, too," I replied in a low voice.

We stopped talking then because we were entering the landing pattern and Rick had to concentrate on getting the plane back down safely.

We rolled to a stop in the same parking space we'd started from, and Rick turned off the engine. Shifting in his seat, he looked at me. "I'd also like to take back what I said about your not having the right stuff, Deena. And I'm really looking forward to being your instructor."

"Oh," I said with a little catch in my throat because of the unexpected compliment.

"Yes." His eyes searched my face. "If you want me to be, that is."

"Oh, I do." I nodded quickly. "I do."

"Good." Rick smiled, and his shoulders kind of relaxed at the same time. "But it'll have to be on Saturdays. That's the only day I teach. See," he began to explain, "I'm still in school—"

"Saturdays will be fine," I interrupted him. "Saturdays will be just great."

Chapter Seven

Mom was in the kitchen again when I arrived home. This time she was busy putting the finishing touches on a chocolate layer cake.

She smiled as she saw my face. Raising the icing-covered spatula in a salute, she said, "I take it that this time I can correctly dub you Pilot Deena? Or is that grin of triumph for some other deed?"

"Yes, yes—I flew. Oh, Mom, I flew!" I ran over and hugged her. "Mom, flying is terrific!" I hugged her again, then let go and whirled around the kitchen table. "Thank you for being the kind of mom you are."

"You mean wonderful?" Mom asked, turning it into a laugh. Then she gave me a curious look. "What do you mean?"

"I mean just that," I said. "A lot of mothers

wouldn't let their daughters go flying. You, well, you encouraged me. Anyway, I just think you're the best mom in the world."

"Well, thank you, honey," Mom said. "But I just think you're kind of high on flying, and want everyone else to be as happy as you are." She stopped, raising an eyebrow. "Hey, did you hear what I said? I made a pun."

"I heard, Mom," I said, groaning. "I heard." Then we both ended up laughing.

"You want a piece of this cake?" Mom asked, still smiling. "With maybe a glass of milk? Then you can sit down and tell me all about your lesson."

"Mom, I'd really love to," I said. "You know I adore chocolate cake almost more than any other food in the universe. And I do want to tell you all about my lesson. But right now I want to get some ideas down for an art project I'm working on. I thought about them on the way home, and I want to get them into my sketchbook before I lose them."

"Of course," Mom answered. "The cake will still be here." She gave me another smile as I hurried through the swinging door and into the hall. Then I ran, two stairs at a time, up to my room.

Turning in my project drawings to Mr. Lander on Monday morning, I knew they were right. When he had flipped through my portfolio and told me he liked them, I felt terrific. I still had a broad smile on my face when I ran into Patty in the hall.

"Wow," she said, taking one look at me. "Looks like the old Deena's back in town. What happened?"

"Patty," I practically yelled, "I did it. I went flying! I took a lesson. Can you believe it?"

"Didn't I tell you that was all you needed?" Patty's face had a smug, knowing look. "That and dumping Senior Boring. But I don't suppose you did that." She shook her head, seeing how my smile had disappeared. "Nope, you didn't."

"Right," I said evenly. "Patty. How can you possibly put flying and Brad together?"

Patty raised one eyebrow slightly. "Just remember, you said that, not me."

I scowled.

"So tell me," she went on. "Have you told Brad about your taking flying lessons yet?"

"Well, no," I admitted.

"Hmmm." Patty folded her arms over her books. "Well, let me know when you do. I'd love to be around. The Fourth of July is my favorite holiday. I absolutely adore fireworks."

"I don't think that's funny."

"Frankly," Patty said, dropping her bantering tone and becoming serious, "I don't either. I like you, Deena. You're my best friend, after all. I hate seeing you hurt. Especially when you're doing it to yourself."

"Don't worry," I assured her. "I know Brad. And I know exactly how to tell him. In fact, I'm planning to tell him this very afternoon." I paused. "Right after I see my counselor."

"What?" Patty looked curious.

"I'm signing up to take business classes this summer."

"Are you serious?" Patty said. She shook her head. "What on earth for? I thought you'd been through this before and decided against that kind of thing."

"It's part of my plan." I put my hand on her arm. "But I don't have time to explain now. I'll tell you later. After I've talked to Brad. But believe me, there won't be any fireworks to watch."

Sitting opposite Brad in a booth in Green's Restaurant after school, I knew that I'd been right. I saw the little smile lines around Brad's eyes deepen when I told him about the classes.

"You'll love word processing, Deena," Brad said excitedly. "And once you've completed the first course, you can go on to programming. Just think, you can learn all about Basic and COBOL . . ."

I let him continue, but I was no longer paying any attention to what he was saying about computers. I was allowing myself to get lost in the depth of his eyes. Brad was so sweet and really understanding. He wouldn't be upset because I hadn't told him about my flying lessons until that day. There'd been other things happening between us, so I hadn't really had the chance. He'd see that. And the reason he would be understanding was because he loved me. Just the way I loved him. Love was wanting the other person to be happy.

"Brad," I said, slipping his name into a pause so that I got his attention, "I have something I want to tell you."

"About word processing?" He gave me an expectant look.

"Not exactly," I said, hesitating.

"What do you mean, not exactly?" He was leaning slightly forward. His hand was no longer holding mine. He'd stopped holding it when he'd started waving his arms about as he was describing the wonders of Basic and COBOL.

"What I mean about it's being sort of to do with word processing is—" I stopped. How was I supposed to explain that I was taking word processing because I wanted him to be happy, so he would be happy, in turn, about my taking flying lessons?

The look on Brad's face was one of total bewilderment. "I'm sorry, Deena. What are you trying to say?"

"I guess, well, I guess what I have to tell you doesn't really have all that much to do with word processing." I hesitated. "I guess it doesn't have anything to do with word processing, actually. I'm taking flying lessons." I started blurting out the rest. "I'm taking them because I won them. I won them because I bought a bunch of raffle tickets at the market. And—and the proceeds went to charity." I closed my eyes. "What I really wanted to win was a typewriter."

"But the prize was flying lessons?" he asked.

"The typewriter was second prize." I opened my eyes and looked at him.

Brad shook his head. "I thought you didn't know how to type."

"I don't." Somehow all this wasn't working out quite the way I'd planned. "I wanted to win the typewriter so I could learn how to type, and then start a part-time business typing papers."

"But you didn't win it?"

"No, of course not," I answered. "I just told you that."

"Yes, I know," Brad said. "I'm only trying to take it all in." He nodded to himself. "You won the flying lessons instead, right?"

"Right."

"I don't believe it!" Now he was shaking his head.

"Brad, I just said—"

"I know what you said," Brad broke in. "But I still can't believe it. Maybe because I don't want to."

"You aren't happy that I won flying lessons?" I asked in a small voice. Oh, why did I bother to ask? I slumped back against the back of the booth. Of course he wasn't happy. Anyone could see that by the look on his face.

"And you've already taken the first lesson?" Brad asked. "Yes, of course, you said you did."

"Saturday." All at once the memory of Saturday slid into my mind. I remembered the feeling of absolute freedom that flying *Quack-Quack* had given me. Suddenly I started to feel defensive about flying. Looking over at Brad, I sat up straight. I was going to stop sounding like a wimp and apologizing because I was doing something I wanted to do. "Yes, I went flying," I repeated. "And I adored every single second. And, what's more, I fully intend to take the rest of the lessons. All nine of them."

"No!" Brad replied almost violently. "You can't!"

"Huh?" I said, surprised by the sudden volume of his voice. "What do you mean *I can't*?"

"Well, uh, just that." Brad sounded flustered as if he'd surprised himself as well. "What I mean is that I don't *want* you to. I don't want—"

"Wait!" I broke in, holding up my hand, palm toward him. "You're telling me I'm not to go flying again because *you* don't want me to?" Leaning across the table, I let my eyes narrow. "Brad Matthews, just where do you think you are? Somewhere in the nineteenth century? In case you haven't noticed, these are the eighties."

"Deena!" Brad said in an almost pleading voice. "Don't look at me like that, please. I know these are the eighties. That wasn't what I meant at all."

"Really?" I replied with a quick toss of my head. "I think I know what the word *can't* means. It's a simple word. It's in every diction-ary." I stopped talking, my mouth still open to say whatever came into my head next. Nothing came out. It was as if my mind had gone into overdrive, then blown a fuse. What was I doing, ranting on like this? This was supposed to be a civilized discussion. I'd gone out of my way to sign up for courses, sacrificing my summer for Brad. Right now he should be saying how happy he was about my flying lessons. We weren't supposed to be having an argument. *Calm down, Deena,* I mentally informed myself. *Calm down and start all over.*

But then I remembered why I'd gone flying in the first place, and I found myself getting heated up all over again. I couldn't help it.

"You know, Brad, I'm beginning to see you in a whole new light." My voice was starting to rise again, but I didn't care. "It's perfectly all right for you to break a date with me—an important date—so you can spend a day with Tabitha Wingford and her stupid computer. But let me try and do something I want to do and it's 'Oh, no, that's all wrong.' Just what am I supposed to do when you're busy with her, sit home and knit you socks?"

"Deena." Brad's face was red. "That's not fair. And you're making a scene."

"You're right—I am," I said. "And you know what? I'm enjoying it."

"Well, I'm not," Brad said, starting to get up.

"Oh, no, Brad," I said, giving him a scathing look. "Don't bother getting up. Let me. I was just about to leave anyway." In one swift move, I pulled Brad's ring from my finger and plopped it down on the tabletop. Then gathering up my things, I slid out of the booth and walked quickly to the door and out of the restaurant.

Soon I was halfway down the next block, my thoughts confused, still going over what had just happened. I was trying to figure out what the argument had really been about. Had it been about my flying? Or had it been about Tabitha and the fact I was more than slightly jealous of her spending time, in school and out, with Brad? She was *so* pretty, *so* smart, and *so* much more right for Brad than I.

All at once there was a hand on my shoulder, and I whirled around to find myself face to face with Brad. "Deena, Deena!" He drew in a breath. "What happened back there? What's really wrong? I mean," he said, taking another breath, "you weren't acting like yourself at all."

"Maybe I really was, for once," I replied, my voice low. Had I been?

"But you didn't give me a chance to really explain. You surprised me with this flying. No, actually you scared me. All I could think of was that flying is awfully dangerous. You hear about small planes crashing all the time. And I don't know what I'd do if I lost you. If something terrible happened to you, I don't think I could handle it."

"Oh," I said softly, my eyes widening. He did care for me. Brad really cared for me. Me—not Tabitha.

"Deena." Brad dropped his ring into my hand, and then he pulled me toward him. "Deena." His voice was low. "Don't you know how much I love you?"

"Yes," I answered, looking into those gray eyes. "I think I do now." But I couldn't say anything more because I was busy being kissed, right there in the middle of the sidewalk of Pinebrook's main street.

Chapter Eight

"These are really excellent, Deena," Mr. Lander said as he looked at my drawings. We were going over them again. He glanced up at me. I was standing opposite him, on the other side of his desk. "I really mean it."

"Thank you," I said, trying to look humble.

"What I still don't understand," he said, scratching thoughtfully at the back of his head, "is the tremendous difference between these and what you turned in the first time. I don't mean to pry, but were you having some sort of personal problem that was affecting your work?" He raised a hand. "No, don't tell me. If you were, it's certainly none of my business. Whatever it was that made the difference, I'm thrilled."

"Really, thank you, Mr. Lander," I felt myself starting to blush. Mr. Lander doesn't give out compliments easily.

"They are so open, so free." He made a flowing gesture with one hand. "The first ones—well, they were good. I mean the mechanical ability was there. But they were so tight." He smiled. "I knew you could do better if I just gave you a chance. And you proved it. You have real talent, Deena."

Now I didn't know what to say. I stood there, wanting to hug myself and grin like an idiot.

Mr. Lander began to stack the sketches, carefully putting them one by one back into my portfolio. "Tell me, Deena," he said, handing me the portfolio. "If you should happen to win the art contest for the ad agency internship, would you be free to accept it? I mean, do you have other plans for the summer?"

I hesitated, stalling with my answer. I couldn't believe it. Was Mr. Lander telling me that I had a chance at winning? It sounded that way. But what should I tell him? That I'd already made plans? That I would fit working at an ad agency into my schedule?

"Oh, I know, Deena," Mr. Lander reached over to give my hand a friendly squeeze. "It's a little early to start thinking about something like that. And I probably shouldn't be giving you this much encouragement. There's so much more to do toward finishing the entries." He let go of my hand to tap the cover of my portfolio. "These are only the start. But they are a good start."

"Do you really think I might have a chance at the internship?" I asked, still feeling the conversation we were having was slightly on the incredible side.

"Yes, Deena." Mr. Lander nodded. "That's exactly what I'm saying. Of course, you must remember that I'm not judging. Agency executives will be doing that. And you do have some rather stiff competition in one of my other classes."

"Then—" I began.

"Deena, I think you're a good student. I also think you have a very definite talent for communicating. Do you understand what I'm saying?"

"I—I think so," I mumbled.

"Good," Mr. Lander said with a nod. "Because I want you to believe me. More than that, I want you to really believe in yourself."

The bell rang, and we both looked up at the clock on the wall.

"You'd better hurry along, Deena. I apologize for keeping you so long. But I did want to let you know I'd looked at the new drawings and how I felt about them." He flashed a rare smile. "Just promise me you won't make any permanent plans for this summer for a while yet."

After I left Mr. Lander's classroom, I began walking slowly down the nearly deserted hallway. I knew I should hurry so that I wouldn't be late to my next class, but I couldn't seem to get my feet to move any faster. My mind was racing, thoughts and emotions stumbling over themselves, one after another, as I tried to sort them out. Finally I gave up and leaned against a nearby wall to steady myself.

I hugged my portfolio to my chest. What if—what if I *did* win? I pictured myself winning. I tried to picture myself accepting the award. But Brad's face got in the way. I shook my head; I pushed his image away. That made me feel guilty. I loved Brad. Brad had told me how much he loved me. How could I go back on my word to him? The answer was simple. I couldn't. With a sigh I forced myself to loosen my grip on my portfolio. Then I pushed myself away from the wall and walked down the hall toward the next class.

Brad is real, I told myself. Winning the art contest was only a dream.

Chapter Nine

Glumly I watched as Rick reduced the speed of the plane, gently pulled back on the wheel, and settled onto the runway in a perfect, bounceless landing. We taxied the length of the strip to *Quack-Quack*'s normal parking space. Rick hit the right brake with his toe, and the plane wheeled into place. He flipped off the ignition, and silence filled the tiny cockpit.

"I was horrible," I said morosely. "Just horrible."

"No, you weren't." Rick turned to face me. I knew his words were meant to soothe me, but there was no way I could believe them.

"I was!" I insisted. "You know it, and I know it," I said, letting my head sink into my hands. Then I forced myself to look directly at him. "What happened? Last week I was fine. You said yourself that I had the stuff necessary to be a good pilot. And this week I practically made us crash."

"Deena!" Rick shook his head, stifling a laugh. "You are definitely exaggerating." The laugh slipped out this time. "I'm sorry," he said. "But, Deena, you hardly put the plane in jeopardy."

"I don't see anything funny." I scowled. "Just what do you see that's so funny?"

"You, Deena." Rick smiled this time. "You're much too hard on yourself." He paused, then leaned back against the door on his side. "Listen. I told you before we went up that a lot of students will do absolutely great on the first day out. Then they'll screw up completely on the second lesson. That does not mean they aren't going to be great again, once they're back on track. Which usually happens on the third lesson. If it helps," he said, a brief smile flickering at the corner of his mouth, "I'll tell you about myself. I messed up royally my second time up. I really did almost crash the plane."

"You did?" I looked into Rick's eyes to see if he was really telling the truth or just trying to make me feel better. I couldn't tell.

"I sure did," Rick told me. "And if you'd like to hear all the gory details, just ask my uncle. Remember? He was my instructor. He'll be thrilled to enlighten you, complete with his own embellishments."

"Honest?" I had to smile.

"Honest!" Rick nodded.

"And you did OK on your third lesson?" I asked.

"Absolutely." Rick held up his hand. "I swear."

I sat for a moment thinking. "All right," I said. "Then I want to go back up. Right now. I want to have my third lesson right now."

Rick's reaction was to laugh. But it was a friendly sympathetic laugh. "I'm sorry, Deena," he said. "It doesn't work that way. The errors you made today were all because you were being too conscious of each thing you were doing. Like trying to break down walking into separate moves." He reached for the door handle. "But trust me, you really did learn today. Honest. Relax. Next week you'll be fine."

"Are you positive?" I demanded.

"Deena!"

"Oh, OK," I said, giving in, but only because he already had one leg out the door.

"Besides," he added, leaning his head back toward me, "I have another lesson in a

*   *   *

When I got home from my lesson, the house was empty. The kitchen was dark, and there wasn't the usual pot of coffee on the stove. Flipping on the overhead light, I saw a note on the refrigerator, stuck there with a fruit-shaped magnet. The note was from Mom, saying she'd gotten a call from the Copper Skillet, the coffee shop she manages part-time, asking her to come down and take over for someone who wasn't feeling well.

I'd really felt like talking to her. I needed to talk to someone, other than Rick, to be reassured that I hadn't done all that badly. It seemed silly, because Mom certainly didn't know anything about flying a plane. But just to hear her say kind, general things would have made me feel better.

I didn't want to stay in the kitchen. The kitchen was always depressing when it was empty. Anyway, I had a lot of work to do on my project. So I got a diet Coke and went upstairs.

Since my sketches had been approved, the next step was to turn them into three final print ads. I also had to sketch out some preliminary ideas for a TV commercial. But that afternoon I would concentrate on the print ads, having come up with a couple of new ideas as I'd been skidding poor *Quack-Quack* around in the sky.

After changing into my at-home clothes, I

switched on the lamp over my worktable, sat down on my stool, and soon became absorbed in my sketches.

It was only when I heard Mom and Dad's voices in the kitchen that I looked over at the window and saw the sun was setting. That's when I remembered that I had a date with Brad to go to the movie at the mall.

I put away the ad I was working on, called down a quick greeting to my parents, and went into the bathroom for a fast shower.

I'd just finished buttoning my cords and pulling a yellow sweater over my head when the doorbell rang. I glanced over at the clock on my bedside table. *Darn*, I thought, I wouldn't have a chance to talk to Mom.

"It's Brad, Deena," Mom called up the stairs.

"OK, I'll be right down."

Going over to the dresser, I picked up a comb and ran it through my hair, trying to straighten some of the curliness from my shower. I added a quick dash of pale coral lipstick before stepping back to survey my looks. *I'll do*, I told myself.

Dashing down the stairs and seeing Brad waiting at the bottom, looking so handsome, I decided to talk to him about what had happened during my lesson. He loved me. He'd reassure me. A little reassurance from him and I'd feel fine again.

I started telling him as he pulled the car away from the curb. I explained about vertical axis and horizontal axis, and about the use of ailerons and rudders, and lift and drag. I got so involved in what I was telling him that I didn't notice that he wasn't responding. We reached an intersection where the light was red, and the way Brad kind of jerked the car to a stop made me look over at him.

What I didn't expect was the way he was looking at me. It was a glare. "You did *what!*"

"I—I made the plane skid," I repeated. "I kept using too much rudder and the plane— Brad, go. The light's turned green."

Brad scowled and pushed down on the gas a lot harder than necessary. The car shot across the street.

"Brad!" I yelled as I found myself being thrown back against the seat. "Stop!"

He did, screeching the car to a halt at the nearest curb. Turning off the motor, he swiveled in his seat. I could see the little muscle along the side of his jaw beginning to work back and forth.

"Repeat what you just told me, Deena. No, no, wait." He threw up his hands, palms facing me. "I really don't want to hear it again. Once was plenty." He leaned toward me. "You promised, Deena. You promised me when I gave you back my ring that you wouldn't go flying again."

"I—I *what*?" I stared. "When did I do that? Sorry, but I don't remember saying anything remotely like that."

"But you did, Deena. You said you loved me. And I told you I wouldn't know what to do if anything happened to you. Planes *are* dangerous. Maybe you didn't say it exactly, but you implied it when you kissed me."

"I thought *you* kissed *me*," I said.

"I did."

"Then?" I couldn't believe his interpretation of that kiss.

"Do you love me? Yes or no?"

"Of course I do," I answered.

"Well, then, if you do, you won't go flying again," Brad finished.

"Why do I get the feeling that this conversation is beginning to sound familiar, Brad? You're trying to play macho, but you've never been a macho person. I don't like people telling me what I can or can't do."

"Deena, please be reasonable," Brad said.

"I am. You're the one who isn't being reasonable. Planes are perfectly safe. It's *people* who sometimes aren't safe." I wanted to stay calm, to talk this all out.

"Well, I guess that stops the argument,"

Brad said, almost sounding smug. "You can hardly be classified as a safe pilot. You've flown what—twice? And already you're telling me you practically crashed the plane."

I closed my eyes, mentally counting to ten. Why did I ever believe I'd get understanding from Brad? I opened my eyes, while working Brad's ring from my finger. "Brad, let's just forget our date tonight. OK?" I took the ring off and put it on the dashboard. "Let's just forget our relationship, period." I started to open the door.

Brad grabbed my arm before I could get out. "What do you think you're doing, Deena?"

"Walking home," I answered. "Isn't it obvious?"

"But you can't!" Brad took a firmer hold. "It's nearly dark. Let me at least drive you home."

"There you go again, Brad," I said calmly as I began to remove his fingers from my arm, one by one. "You're telling me what to do again. Don't you get it yet? Or is it simply that you can't hear yourself?" I felt so clear-headed. I wasn't even angry. I glanced around at the perfectly safe neighborhood. "I'll be fine, Brad. I *want* to walk home by myself. This is Pinebrook; it's hardly a crime-ridden town."

This time I managed to slip out of the car. But before I left I leaned down briefly. "Good night, Brad." I hesitated. "No, not good night, goodbye." And I shut the car door.

Chapter Ten

Naturally, the first thing Patty noticed Monday morning was that I was no longer wearing Brad's ring. I steeled myself, waiting for whatever it was she was going to say. But she took one look at my face and said nothing. Not even one little remark about my new-found wisdom. I guess my unhappiness really showed.

By lunchtime I could see she was about to burst with questions. Especially since Brad and Tabitha were sharing a table and computer printouts near us. I decided to fill her in before she threatened to self-destruct.

"You were right, Patty," I said, trying to keep my voice objective. "Brad Matthews is not right for me." I hesitated as I remembered Brad's last kiss. "And it isn't because he's totally boring, the way you thought."

"So, what *is* the reason for your newly naked finger?" Patty asked, tipping her head and looking first at me, then rather pointedly over at the table where Brad and Tabitha sat.

"No," I shook my head. "Not her either. Though I have to admit she definitely annoys me with her perfectness."

"Perfectness?"

"Oh, you know. She has perfect hair, a perfect figure, a perfect brain."

"I don't know about that," Patty said, looking across the room and appraising Tabitha. "She does have pretty hair. I have to admit that. But, personally, I think she's too skinny. Skinny is out. It's not healthy. As for her brain, I think that's highly overrated. Just because she's in the business club and a lot of other school activities doesn't mean she's smart. It only means she's hyperactive."

"Oh, Patty," I said, laughing. "Thank you for trying to cheer me up. But, as I said, Tabitha Wingford is not my problem."

"Well, what is then?" Patty leaned forward. "I am positively dying of curiosity."

"It's the most basic problem," I answered her. "Brad Matthews is a chauvinist." And I explained about Brad's reaction to my winning, and using, the flying lessons. "And on Saturday, he *told* me I wasn't to go flying again because *he* didn't want me to."

"Why?" Patty asked with an astonished stare.

"He said he didn't want anything to happen to me. That flying a plane is too dangerous."

"Really?" Patty said thoughtfully. "Actually that sounds as if he honestly cares about you. So, what's wrong with that?"

"Don't you get it, Patty? Brad was *telling* me what to do. Look, I'm not exactly a feminist. But I realize now that I don't want a guy treating me as if I don't have the brains to make it across the street without his help."

"Um-hmm," Patty mused. "Well, I'm not saying I've changed my mind about Brad. He's still dull. But it seems to me he's simply being protective because he loves you. That sounds pretty romantic to me. And you're the one who's always talking up how you want more romance. So here it is, and now you don't want it. I don't get you."

"Being protective is one thing." I shook my head in exasperation. Why didn't she understand? "Outright demanding is another. And that's what Brad did, demand that I give up flying. Well, actually his exact words were, 'if you love me, you'll give up flying.' "

"And you chose flying?" Patty stared in disbelief. "But that's wild. You've been going

99

with Brad for months. You've only been flying twice. Wow! Flying must have some strong attraction."

"I give up." I threw up my hands. "You don't listen any better than Brad. Whether I love flying more than I love Brad isn't the point. It's that he demanded that I choose between the two."

"I thought I was listening," Patty said, sounding slightly hurt.

"Oh, Patty, I'm sorry," I apologized. "I guess I'm still feeling a little hostile."

"That's OK," Patty acknowledged graciously. "I understand. As far as Brad Matthews is concerned, you and he are yesterday's news. That much I accept." She picked up half a grilled cheese sandwich from her plate. "Tell me about this Rick character. He sounds cute."

"Patty!" I was astonished. "How can you dismiss one guy and ask about another in the very same breath?"

Patty swallowed. "Easy," she said, shrugging. "That's the way I handle life. I don't allow myself to fall into the potential trap of a boyless situation. Lose one, get another is my motto." She waved her sandwich at me. "And it works, too. You'll never find me walking around school looking totally depressed the way you are right now."

"I'm not depressed," I insisted. "I'm still angry, that's all." I frowned slightly, turning my head so I no longer had to see Brad and Tabitha. "Besides, it's Monday, and I just don't feel like being at school today."

"Sure." Patty nodded. "Tell me about it, Deena. You like school, and you know it. Now stop letting that dumb duo over there get to you." She dropped the last of her sandwich on her plate and leaned on her elbows. "Now tell me all about Rick. I think he sounds just like the kind of guy you need to make you forget all about boring Brad."

"Patty, get real," I protested. "Rick Gillian is my instructor. That's all. Besides, he's so much older."

"How much older?"

"Oh, I don't know." Rick's face flashed into my mind. "Just older."

"Well, how much?" Patty said. "Three, four years? Ten?"

"Well, OK, maybe a year," I admitted. Then I hurried on. "But he seems older. He's very mature. He's a senior at Danville High. And you know how the kids at Danville always look so much more sophisticated. They're from the city, and it shows."

"Maturity, huh?" Patty made a tent of her hands and peered at me over the top. "I thought you liked maturity. Now you're putting that down, too. Brad's suddenly too romantic. This guy's too mature. You know something? I don't think you know what you want."

"This is a different kind of maturity," I insisted. "It's more like I said, sophistication. Oh, I don't know. You'd have to meet him to understand."

"Ohhh." Patty smiled mischievously. "Does that mean you'll introduce me?"

"Patty! You're incorrigible," I said, laughing.

"Yeah!" she answered, grinning widely. "But life is so much more fun that way." She sobered and put a hand on my arm. "You know I'm kidding, don't you?"

"Of course I do," I said. "You're my best friend. Besides, I also happen to know you're still madly in love with Richard." I winked at her. "Aren't you? Or are you just trying to line up the next one?"

"Deena!" A second later Patty said, "Hey, this place is a little crowded. If you know what I mean." She glanced toward the table where Brad was still sitting with Tabitha. "Why don't we get out of here and go get ice cream from the snack bar?"

I nodded to show I understood what she meant. I looked at the green salad I'd toyed with while she'd eaten her grilled cheese sand-

wich. Yuck. "Sure," I said. "I'd love ice cream."
I pushed my chair out and stood up. "You did
say skinny was out, didn't you?"

Patty stood up too. "Yes." This time the
glance toward Tabitha was open. "Skinny is
definitely out!" She picked up her tray. "Shall
we go, *best friend*?"

"The sooner, the better, *best friend*," I
replied, picking up my own tray.

Propping the three finished print ads
against the wall at the back of my worktable, I
spotlighted them with my desk lamp. It was
almost eleven o'clock on Thursday night, and
the ads were due in the morning. I'd worked
hard on them every night that week.

I tried to see them as Mr. Lander would, as
an art teacher would. Then I tried to look at
them from the viewpoint of a commercial art
director.

We had each been assigned a different
product to work on. Mine was for a made-up
bicycle company. I had to invent a logo and
name. I'd called my product the Fast Ten Bicycle. For the theme for the ads I decided to use
bicycle touring.

I'd depicted three different countries—
France, Holland, and the United States. I'd
gotten my inspiration from my first time in
the air. Each ad was drawn as if the scene

were being viewed from high up in a small plane. A lone rider was shown traveling through a landscape from each country: France had rows of grapes in a vineyard; Holland had windmills; the United States was a New England landscape with the rider on a narrow black road winding through masses of colorful fall trees.

I pulled my knees up and rested my head on them, staring at the three ads. Actually, they weren't bad at all. I considered them among the best work I'd ever done. My style was airy and free. The colors were clear and inviting; they made even me want to enter the scene with the solitary bicycle rider.

My only concern was that I hadn't included any real copy. I'd done the company name, Fast Ten Bicycle, in white script in the upper right-hand corner. I liked the simplicity of the statement, but was it enough? Would the advertising executives think I didn't understand that the idea behind the ad was to get people to buy?

Well, I thought, it was a bit late to consider that now. The assignment was due in the morning. I hoped my original intuition about my campaign had been correct. I stretched as I stood up, my muscles complaining, switched off the lamp, and fell into bed. I don't even remember dreaming.

On the way to school I had felt confident, but when I saw the stacks of other portfolios on the corner of Mr. Lander's desk, my confidence began to fade. How many other students thought they, too, had a chance at winning the contest? How many had the talent to win? Mr. Lander had told me he thought I stood a good chance. But he wasn't a judge.

After turning in my portfolio, I walked out into the hall and bumped into a guy. He reached out to grab the books that were sliding out of my arms. His hands looked familiar.

"Oh—uh, thanks," I mumbled. "I'm sorry." I looked up to see Brad. "Hi," I added weakly.

"Hi, Deena." I could see him start to smile. Then the smile faded. "How are you?"

"Oh, fine," I answered. "Just fine. And you?"

"Fine," Brad replied. "Really fine."

We stared uncomfortably at each other. I couldn't think of anything else to say, and I had a feeling that neither could he.

"Well, I've got to go," Brad said after a few seconds. "I'll see you around."

"Yeah," I answered. "See you." And I watched until he disappeared into the crowd.

The rest of the day I thought about having

run into Brad. That afternoon, walking home with Patty, I continued to think about Brad, remembering the look in his eyes. It hadn't been cold or angry. It had been, well, almost warm. The more I thought, the surer I was that he'd wanted to say more but hadn't because he wasn't sure how I'd take it.

"Patty," I said hesitantly, "I've been thinking. Maybe I should stop taking flying lessons."

Patty stopped in the middle of the sidewalk and turned to stare at me. "What are you talking about? I thought you said you loved flying. Why would you want to give it up?"

"Well, see, Brad—" I began.

"Brad!" Patty yelped. "Didn't you tell me at the beginning of the week that Brad was absolute poison? That he was a total chauvinist? That he was treating you like a helpless little girl?"

"I know," I agreed. "But you're the one who pointed out to me that the only reason he acted the way he did was because he cared about me and was afraid I'd get killed."

"True," Patty said, beginning to walk again.

"So, I started thinking this afternoon that the whole breakup had been my fault. That it never would have happened if I'd gone ahead and told him about winning the raffle in the first place. Maybe it *was* thoughtless of me not to consult with him about taking the lessons. I can see, now, that it was telling him after I'd done it that upset him so much," I finished.

"Uh-huh, maybe," Patty said. "But I don't think you should forget the fact that you'd never have taken that lesson if Brad hadn't walked out on your picnic in the first place."

"Maybe he never wanted to go on the picnic. I know he wasn't exactly enthusiastic about it," I said, defending him.

"Then he should have said so when you first invited him, instead of making up some stupid excuse about a date with a computer."

"Well . . ." I hesitated, looking for something reasonable to say.

"Listen, Deena," Patty said. "You know I'm right. You've already broken up with Brad. Now leave it that way." She put her hand on my arm. "Take my advice. Go out to the airport tomorrow and take another lesson. Get cozy with that adorable instructor. What's his name?"

"Rick," I said. "Rick Gillian."

"A cute name," Patty said. "Yeah, I like the name Rick. Deena and Rick. It sounds nice."

"Forget it," I told her. "How many times do I have to say it? Rick Gillian is my instructor. My *instructor*."

"Good," Patty replied her eyes twinkling. "He's your instructor. So let him instruct. Take a lesson tomorrow. All right?"

"OK," I said. "OK!" I smiled. "Just stop pushing." But as I walked the rest of the way home, thoughts of Brad stayed with me, not those of Rick.

Chapter Eleven

Saturday had become my favorite day of the week because of flying. I stopped worrying about my awful second lesson. I realized it was just as Rick had said, the second time was simply something to get through. Rick had also said that once in a while a student made terrific strides in the third lesson, as if he'd suddenly crammed several hours into one.

Well, I was one of those students. My third lesson was terrific. Walking away from the plane with Rick to log in my third hour, I felt so excited that I wanted to jump up and down and yell about how great I was feeling. But I didn't. I tried to be cool. "Are you really sure I did OK?" I asked, turning to Rick.

"You're fishing, Deena," he said, smiling.

"No, I'm not," I insisted.

"Well, this is the third time you've asked." Slipping a friendly arm around my shoulders, he said, "For the third time then—you did brilliantly." He squeezed me, nearly lifting me off the pavement with the strength of his hug. "If you hadn't done as well as you did, I never would have allowed you to land the plane by yourself."

I lost my cool and shouted, "I really did do it, didn't I? I still can't believe it!"

"Believe me, you did. All I did was talk you through the landing."

"But I was so sure you had your hand on the wheel the whole time."

"Only until we reached base leg. Then I let go. You were so busy you never noticed."

"You know what I feel like doing?" I said suddenly.

"What?" He smiled, his arm still around my shoulders. "What do you feel like doing, Deena?"

"Celebrating!" I said. "I want to celebrate."

"You know," he said, cocking his head to one side, "that sounds like a great idea."

"Huh?"

"Sure!" He smiled decisively. "Why not!" His face was very close to mine, and I could feel his breath warm on my face. "I've got the next couple of hours off today. And it's almost lunchtime. How about if I buy you a hangar special to celebrate your first official landing?"

"A hangar special?" I asked, looking back into those eyes. "What's a hangar special?"

"Say yes. Then you'll find out."

"Yes," I said and laughed.

The hangar special turned out to be the Airport Cafe's version of a super-duper deluxe hamburger. It had everything one could possibly ask for on a hamburger, plus a lot more, like chopped peanuts and crumbled bacon. It was very, very messy. But also very, very good.

Rick ordered them to take out. We took them, along with french fries and soft drinks, to a grassy knoll near the end of the runway. While we ate, we watched the planes take off.

The air was warm so Rick took off his jacket to put on the ground for me to sit on. At one point he reached over and gently wiped my chin with his napkin. "Mustard," he explained. But his hand did linger for a long moment after he'd finished wiping.

Walking back with me to the car, Rick made a suggestion. "I was thinking, Deena. Maybe we could see each other sometime. You know, away from the airport."

I was too surprised to answer, so I simply nodded my head to show him I liked the idea.

As we walked on, I waited for him to make the next move, to invite me somewhere—like to a movie. When he didn't say anything, I began to wonder if he'd seen me nod. I felt stupid. Was he thinking I'd meant I didn't like the idea because I hadn't said anything?

I wanted to reassure him, to tell him I'd meant yes. I just hadn't said it out loud. By that time, though, it seemed too late. We'd already reached the side of the car. He leaned one arm against the top as I unlocked the door with my keys. Then he reached down and opened the door for me. I slid in, and he shut the door, making sure it was secure.

He stood there as I started the car. What was I supposed to do? Jump back out of the car and throw myself at him, saying, "Yes, Rick. I'd love a date with you. Where'll we go? And how soon?" Well, that was something I couldn't do. I was too busy absorbing the sub-tle shift in our relationship, from instructor and pupil to what? I was sure I wanted to go out with Rick. Yet the thought scared me, and more than just a little bit.

He stood there politely, waiting for me to back the car out before he went back to the field. I couldn't leave without saying some-thing more. I rolled down the window and stuck my head out. "Thanks again for the hangar special," I said over the sound of the car engine. I searched for something else to say. "I thought it was great."

"You're welcome," Rick replied. "I'm glad you liked it."

Had I imagined it, or did his voice sound impersonal again? As if he was sorry he'd asked me for the date? I waited, hoping he might say something else. But when he didn't, I rolled up the window and backed out of the space. I glanced over at Rick, lifting my hand in a small wave. He returned the wave. But that was all it was, just an answering wave. There was nothing left for me to do but drive away.

Chapter Twelve

I worked all day Sunday completing the TV storyboard for the contest. I was so happy with it that I decided to show it to Patty Monday morning before turning it in. "It's supposed to be for a fifteen-second TV commercial," I explained.

"Well—I think it's adorable, Deena," Patty said hesitantly. "But I didn't know you were into doing cartoons."

"That's what a storyboard is, Patty," I said, trying not to sound impatient. I pointed to the series of pictures. "See, this gives you the highlights of a piece of finished film."

"Ahh," Patty nodded with understanding. "Then these will be real actors, not cartoon figures."

"Right." I tapped the first picture. "It

opens here, with a girl riding her bike along a country road." I moved my finger to the second frame. "Then this plane comes into the story. I made it an old-fashioned plane because it seems a little more romantic. Besides, that way I could show the pilot's face." I smiled. "And I gave him one of those long, white scarves because I thought that was romantic, too."

"Does Rick wear one of those?" Patty asked with a smile.

"Of course not," I answered.

"What does he wear?"

"He dresses just like any ordinary guy," I said with a hint of exasperation.

"Like what did he wear last week?"

"I don't remember," I answered, feeling flustered that the conversation had taken this turn. "A yellow and white shirt, jeans, and a gray jacket." I blushed as I remembered sitting on that jacket and having Rick wipe mustard from my chin.

"Sounds like you remember pretty well, for not remembering," Patty said teasingly.

"Patty!" I started to pull the storyboard away from her. "Are you interested in what I did for the contest? Or are you just interested in making me feel dumb?"

"Sorry," she apologized, pulling the sheet

of cardboard back. "Let me see. I'll be serious now and tell you exactly what I think."

"All right," I said, glaring at her to convince her I really did want her opinion. "So this pilot is in love with the girl. But she's run away from him. And he uses the plane to find her. It's in this second frame that he finds her. He drops a note to her. It's a note declaring his love."

Patty bent her head to read the copy on the note, which was in the next frame. She squinted at the small print and read it aloud. "I love you, and your Fast Ten Bicycle!"

"I know," I said, wagging my head. "It's corny. But I had to get the product name in there somewhere."

"I guess," Patty said, shrugging.

"Then we come down to the final picture. There they are, standing together on a grassy hill. He's landed his plane. I put it in the background. But her bicycle is lying in a prominent position in the foreground. And as they melt into each other's arms, the announcer says, 'Ride a Fast Ten and find the love of your life.' At the same time, the words Fast Ten Bicycle zoom up and fill the screen over the kiss."

"Oh, Deena," Patty said. "I know I made fun of the note, but I really do love what you've

117

done. You've got to win. I know you will. I just do."

"Thank you," I answered graciously. "I only wish I was so sure. There are so many different factors involved in advertising. Simply being cute, or pretty, or interesting doesn't always make it."

"Well, I know *you'll* make it," she announced firmly. "You're my best friend. I dare anyone else to win."

"Can I send you along with this to the judges?" I asked.

But she was looking at the storyboard again, holding it up close so she could study something on it. "You know, Deena," she said, glancing up at me, "this girl on the bicycle looks a lot like you. Did you do that on purpose? Or perhaps it was subconscious." She bent her head to study something else. "Then this would be Rick. Right?" She looked at me and grinned. "Is he as handsome in person as he is here?"

"Don't be ridiculous!" I replied. Taking the storyboard from her, I looked for myself. I studied the figure of the pilot. There might be a slight resemblance, a bit around the jaw. And I'd given him dark, wavy hair. But, I told myself, it could be anyone. "Wrong," I declared, shoving the storyboard into my portfolio. "They are simply made-up figures I used to illustrate my product. That's all."

"Right," Patty replied. "Tell me about it, Deena!" She laughed lightly. "Face it, girl. You've fallen for the guy. And from what I see here, I don't blame you. I have a feeling he's the right one for you."

Patty's words came back to me in the middle of my lesson the following Saturday. We were out in the practice area. I'd just finished a turn. Straightening the plane out, I glanced at Rick. He was looking forward. I compared him to the pilot I'd drawn in my storyboard. Patty hadn't been far off; there was a definite resemblance between Rick and my make-believe pilot.

"Watch that left aileron, Deena," Rick cautioned. "It's beginning to dip."

I jumped at being caught off guard for a moment. "Sorry," I said contritely. I vowed to concentrate on my flying. Thank goodness he hadn't seen me staring at him.

"Time's about up, Deena," Rick said easily. "I think we'd better head for home."

"OK," I answered, promising myself I wouldn't think of anything but flying until we were back on the ground. I wouldn't even look at Rick until then. Banking the plane so we were headed west, I found the highway below and began to follow it back to the airport.

"You did all right today," Rick said. "Learning how to pull out of a stall can be tricky. But you picked it right up. You didn't panic, and you followed my directions. In fact," he added, "because of that I think you should be able to solo pretty soon."

"Solo!" I yelped. "You mean go up on my own? By myself?"

"That's what solo means," Rick replied with a small laugh. "Listen, Deena, you're going to have to do it sometime. That's the whole idea of lessons. Otherwise, you could hire me as your permanent pilot. You wouldn't need to take lessons at all."

"B-but *not* next time?" I stammered, my mouth becoming dry at the thought.

"No," Rick replied. "Not next time. But soon. First I have to be sure you really are capable of taking the plane into the air and getting back on the ground safely. So, I'm planning to let you spend next week practicing touch and gos."

"You mean takeoffs and landings?"

"Yes. Your takeoffs are fine. But you still have a tendency to bounce when you land. I want to be sure you're going to come back to me in one piece." He paused, and his next words slid over me like a soft caress. "I don't want anything happening to my favorite student."

Favorite student. I smiled to myself. Had he really said that? I kept my eyes forward.

"There's something else I had in mind for next week, too."

"Oh," I asked, thinking it was something about the lesson. "What?"

"I was hoping you'd go to a party with me?"

"A party!" Startled, I accidentally jerked the control wheel to the right. The plane dipped. I hurried to correct the dip, and I overcorrected. I corrected once more and finally got us flying even again. When I looked over at Rick, he was laughing.

"You'd better watch it," he said. "With all that wing waggling, someone will think you're signaling for help."

"Well, you startled me," I said. "Did you really invite me to a party?"

"Yes." Rick smiled, "You *did* say, last week, you'd go out with me, didn't you?"

"Yes," I assured him. "I did."

"Good." He relaxed in his seat. "Don't worry, it's not a fancy party. Just a little get-together with some friends of mine. I think you'll like them."

"I hope they'll like me," I said.

"Does that mean you accept my invitation?"

"Yes, Rick." I turned my head just long enough to smile. "I'd love to go to a party with you."

I was still feeling high about Rick's invitation when I pulled into our driveway. So high that I didn't notice Brad's car parked at the curb until I was halfway down the driveway, walking to the front walk. Then I saw it.

As I approached the walkway, Brad stood up. He'd been waiting for me on our front porch swing. He was holding out a small bouquet of pink carnations.

"Hi," he said. "I hope I remembered right. Pink is your favorite color, isn't it?"

"Well, yes—" I stared. "It is." Flustered, I accepted the flowers, lifting them to my face. "They're beautiful." Baby's breath and ferns had been mixed in with the pink carnations. "Thank you. But why?"

"They're meant as an apology for the way I acted," Brad answered in an embarrassed voice.

I wasn't sure if he was embarrassed because he was apologizing, or because bringing flowers to a girl was something new for him.

"Oh?"

"Yes," he said. "I guess I was a real stuffed jerk."

A stuffed jerk? I had to smile. I'd never heard anyone call himself that before.

"Does that smile mean I'm forgiven?" Brad asked, misinterpreting my reaction.

"Oh, Brad—" I'm not sure what I intended to say next because Brad broke in.

"What I want to know is, can we give our relationship one more try?" He reached out to touch my arm. "I was thinking maybe we could go out tonight on a trial date?"

"A date?" I bit my lower lip. How could I accept a date with Brad when I'd already accepted a date with Rick for next week? I couldn't date two boys at once. I looked down at the beautiful arrangement of flowers in my hand. How could I turn down a date with someone who'd just brought me flowers? I'd never received flowers before. It was such a romantic gesture.

"Where'd you want to go?" I asked.

Brad ran his hand through his hair in a nervous gesture. "We never saw that movie at the mall. Unless, of course, you've seen it since."

"I haven't," I answered.

"Well?" He looked almost pleading. "A movie is a good first date. We could go for sodas after."

"A movie, Brad. Just a movie. Let's save the sodas for another time."

"Then you'll go!" Brad let out a sigh.

"A movie sounds like fun," I answered.

Chapter Thirteen

Gently I pulled one of the pink blossoms from the vase on my dresser. I touched the edges with my fingertips. They were brown. I should have thrown the flowers out several days before. Well, maybe I'd do that the next day. I would press one to keep, though. I picked one out. Carrying it over to the window, I leaned against the frame and looked out.

I twirled the flower between my fingers and thought about Brad. He'd changed so much in the last week. Bringing me that bouquet had been only the beginning. At the movie he'd been attentive and thoughtful and never mentioned computers once. He'd remained attentive all week long. He was being everything I'd secretly longed for in a boyfriend.

We were even going on our long-overdue picnic the next day, Sunday. And it had been his idea, not mine. He was even bringing the food, and all I had to do was look pretty.

But all of this was making me crazy. I wanted to tell Brad to stop it. I wanted him to go back to being the old Brad.

Several times during the week I'd almost told him that. But then I'd look at him and see how hard he was trying. And instead of asking him to just be himself, I'd remain silent. We'd be alone the next day, and I'd try to talk to him then.

Looking out the window, I saw long purple clouds at the top of the mountains. The picnic might be rained out. I watched as the sun slipped behind the clouds, and I lifted the flower to my nose to sniff once more.

What was I doing, thinking about Brad when I should have been getting ready for my date with Rick Gillian. I should have started getting ready ages ago. I wanted Rick to see how pretty I could look when I wasn't in my flying clothes, and I wanted his friends to approve of me.

An hour later I wasn't sure if I'd chosen the right thing to wear. I'd tried on three outfits but thought my pale blue, pleated pants seemed right with the angora and lambswool sweater. But were the short sleeves too short?

What about the scooped neck? Was it too dressy? Or not dressy enough? I knew I was spending far too much time worrying.

I was still wondering about my outfit when Rick arrived. I opened the front door to let him in, and the look in his eyes instantly reassured me. I knew I looked good.

Still I was glad that when we were alone in his car, he gave me a warm smile and said, "Did I tell you how much I like the way you look tonight?"

"Not yet," I answered coyly.

"Ah, a terrible oversight," he said, teasing me. "Well, let me take care of that right now. Deena, you look terrific."

"Then I'm dressed all right? I mean for the party with your friends?"

Rick gave a little laugh, then flashed a quick smile in my direction. "You never stop fishing, do you, Deena? OK, I'll say it again. You look great. You look so great that I'm almost afraid to introduce you to a couple of my friends." His voice was still teasing. "I'll probably have to fight to keep them from taking you away from me."

I decided to do my own teasing. "Don't worry, Rick. I'm definitely your girl for the evening."

There was a long beat. Then Rick asked

softly, his voice sounding completely serious. "Just for tonight?"

The question took me by surprise. I didn't know how to answer. So I didn't. I looked out the window and made some stupid comment about how clear the evening was. After that, we didn't say much to each other, Rick seemed to withdraw.

As Rick pulled into the parking lot of a large apartment complex, I asked, "Who lives here?"

"Cindy Peters," Rick replied. His voice was no longer teasing or soft. It had a slight edge to it. I'd done it again, pushed him away without meaning to.

"Is this where the party is?" I asked, trying not to show I'd noticed the change in him.

"Yes," Rick replied abruptly as he jockeyed into a parking space.

But by the time we'd climbed the outside stairs to the second level of one of the buildings, Rick's grim look had started to fade. When the door opened and a pretty red-haired girl screamed "Rick!" and threw her arms around him, it vanished altogether.

"Rick," she said, untangling herself from him, "how great of you to come." She looked over at me. "And *you* must be Deena."

"Yes," I said, smiling slightly.

"I'm Cindy Peters," she said. "I'm your

hostess tonight." Then she put a possessive arm around Rick's waist and hugged him. "And Rick, here, is just about my favorite boy in the world." She winked up at Rick and gave me a conspiratorial grin. "Other than Johnny, that is."

"Ohh?" I wasn't sure what else to say. Who was Johnny?

"Johnny's here?" Rick asked, surprised.

"Yes." Cindy nodded happily. She turned to me to explain. "Johnny's my boyfriend. Rick and he and I all grew up together. But Johnny's always been one year ahead. And now he's a freshman at the university in Las Vegas. He doesn't get home that often."

"Oh," I said again, this time relieved. "Well, I'm glad for you."

Cindy rolled her eyes. "I can hardly wait until I'm a freshman next year and we can be together again all the time. I—" She stopped talking as the door bell sounded. "Oops! Looks like more bodies are here." She looked up at Rick. "There are drinks in the kitchen. Why don't you and Deena go help yourself. There's food, too, whenever you want some." She turned away to open the door.

"Come on," Rick said. "I know the way to the kitchen. The apartment's not all that big."

As we moved toward the kitchen, I glanced at the people crowded into the living room. I was surprised to see they looked like the kids I knew. I'd thought they'd be different somehow. After all, they were the Danville crowd, from the city. Shouldn't they be more sophisticated? I smiled to myself as I realized I'd chosen just the right thing to wear. Two other girls had on pleated pants just like mine. Only the colors were different. And four girls had sweaters similar to mine. I suddenly felt a lot more comfortable.

Rick pushed open the swinging door to the kitchen area. Obviously he felt at home. As I watched him fill the glasses with ice from the refrigerator, a tiny question crossed my mind. Cindy was Johnny's girl now. But had she ever been Rick's? As she had said, the three of them had been friends for a long time. And Cindy was terribly pretty.

Rick interrupted my thoughts by turning to ask what I wanted to drink. Large bottles of soft drinks stood on the counter. I pointed to one. Rick smiled and poured it.

What was I doing, speculating about other girls who may, or may not, have been in Rick's life? How dumb. This was, after all, our first date. We hadn't even kissed.

Rick handed me my glass. I took it, tinkling the cubes against the sides. I had just realized how alone we were in the kitchen. It made me feel nervous, and that was dumb, too. We'd been alone before, cooped up in *Quack-Quack*'s tiny cockpit. But this was different. Rick was standing close to me as I leaned against the counter. His fingers weren't touching mine, but I could feel the soft hairs along the back of his hand brush against my hand. I quit staring into my drink and looked up. His dark eyes looked into mine. Slowly he bent his head toward me, his mouth coming closer and closer. I lifted and turned my chin. I closed my eyes, expecting his mouth to meet mine at any second—

Suddenly the door crashed open, and I heard a loud male voice yell excitedly, "Rick— Rick!"

Startled, my eyes flew open. Rick was being clasped around the shoulders by a giant-sized guy. He was at least a foot taller than Rick and weighed at least forty pounds more. He had bright red hair, and if I hadn't already guessed that he was Johnny, I would have thought he was Cindy's brother. Rick wasn't being crushed, though. He was doing a lot of hugging back. Cindy was standing beside him.

"Come on, Deena." She held out a hand, took my arm, and pulled me past the guys. "Rick won't know you're here for at least ten minutes. Maybe more. Honestly, you'd think they hadn't seen each other in years." Out of the kitchen she said, "Now I'll be a proper hostess and introduce you around. OK?"

I nodded. Without Rick beside me, the nervousness of being alone in a crowd of strangers started to take over. Cindy was still holding onto my arm. She pulled me over to the nearest group, two couples sharing the couch.

They turned out to be very nice. One of the girls complimented me on my sweater and asked where I'd bought it. I confessed it was from a small shop in Pinebrook, where I lived. She said she thought that it would be great to live just down the hill from a ski resort. I told her that I'd always envied the Danville people and their city life. We both laughed.

Cindy pulled me away. As we left the girl told me to come back and tell her how to find the sweater shop because she wanted to come over sometime and see what else they had. I promised I would.

Everyone else was just as friendly. By the time we'd made the rounds, Rick was back by my side, carrying two plates heaped with food. "I thought I'd better bring a peace offering," he said, grinning. We found a spot near the fireplace to sit and eat.

The evening went fast after that—too fast. We played charades, and later Johnny built a fire in the fireplace. Cindy turned the lights down so that only the firelight filled the room, flickering over everyone's faces. Rick and I were sharing a large floor cushion. His arm was around my shoulders, and it seemed natural to lay my head down on his shoulder. A little bit later, it seemed just as natural for him to move his head just enough so that he could gently kiss my cheek.

We drove back to Pinebrook in companionable silence. Rick walked me up to my front door and took both my hands and pulled me close. "I'll tell you a small secret," he said, his voice low. "I don't usually like parties all that much. But tonight, I wanted the party to last forever. Then I wouldn't have to bring you home." Before I could tell him I felt the same way, he let go of my hands, put his arms around me and took up where he'd left off in Cindy's kitchen. It was a kiss with such a gentle warmth that I knew I'd always remember it.

Chapter Fourteen

Bars of early-morning sun fell across my face, waking me gently. I remembered the kiss Rick and I had shared, and I smiled happily and snuggled down into my blankets for another five minutes of sleep. Then all at once I sat up in bed to check the clock on my bed-side table.

Brad and I were going on our picnic that morning, and I had to get ready. The hands on the clock read five minutes to eight. I still had plenty of time. Relieved, I sank back against the pillows. I was wide awake, though, and lay there, thinking about Brad.

I'd never told Brad about my date with Rick. In the past week Brad had acted more like a real boyfriend than he had during the entire time we had gone together. I couldn't bring myself to say anything to him about Rick because I was afraid of his reaction.

Once more I'd kept a secret from Brad. What did that say about our relationship— about my half of the relationship? If I couldn't feel comfortable enough to be totally honest with him, what kind of a future could we have together? Could I still be in love with Brad? What about Rick?

I looked out the window at the clear sky. No chance of rain. It was a beautiful day for a picnic. But would it turn out to be a romantic one?

"So," I said, swiveling around in the front seat of Brad's car in order to look into the back, "what did you bring to eat?" I didn't see a picnic basket, only a large, brown paper bag.

"I wasn't really sure what to bring," Brad confessed. "I haven't been on a real picnic since I was little. I tried to remember what my mother used to fix, but all I could think of was deviled eggs."

"Oh, good," I said, attempting to sound enthusiastic.

"Gee, Deena," Brad said, sounding apologetic, "I didn't know. I didn't include them."

"But—"

"Well, the only reason I remembered the

deviled eggs was because that was the part of the picnic I always hated most."

Oh, boy, I thought to myself. *We're really off to a fantastic start. The first thing he's telling me is what he hates most.*

Brad went on. "They were always smashed and gooey by the time my mother unwrapped them. The other thing I hated was that bugs always landed on whatever I was about to eat, just as I was putting it in my mouth." He fell silent.

I thought about asking him what he *did* like. But I was afraid to—afraid his answer might end our picnic before we even got out of town and into the country. Instead I asked, "Well, what did you bring? It smells good."

"I stopped by your mom's place on the way to your house and had a lunch made up."

"My mom's place?" I asked trying to understand.

"You know," Brad said. "The Copper Skillet. I figured someone there would know what you liked to eat. I wanted to get your favorites."

"Which are?"

"Ham and cheese sandwiches on rye bread, potato salad, and chocolate cake. Oh, yes, and lots of kosher pickles."

"Kosher pickles?" I stared, not believing he'd really gotten them. "Garlic pickles?"

"Uh-huh," Brad answered happily. "The counter girl said you always order them."

"Right," I said. "I love them." I slumped back into the seat. *But not on a romantic picnic*, I thought.

"We're almost out of town," Brad said, getting my attention. After his announcement about the pickles, I'd given up conversation and stared moodily out of the window. "Did you want to pick the place for our picnic? Or should I keep on driving until we get to the county park?"

"The county park?" I tried not to sound too disappointed. "Brad, the county park is always full of little kids running around."

"Yes, but it has picnic tables," Brad replied, slipping momentarily into his old practical self. Then he added, "But you have someplace definite in mind, don't you, Deena?" He smiled. "Just name it, and we'll drive there."

"Well," I said hesitantly, "I sort of thought Brink's Meadow would be nice. There's this little stream that runs through it." I remembered something. "Did you happen to bring a blanket to sit on?"

"Didn't I tell you I'd take care of everything?" Brad said, almost too pleasantly.

"Yes, you did." I sighed. "You certainly did." This was turning out to be about as romantic as hamburgers and fries at the A & W drive-in.

"Did you say something, Deena?" Brad glanced over with a questioning look.

"Oh"—I forced myself to smile—"I just said you certainly took care of everything."

"Well, I hope so."

I nodded, then slid down in my seat. I turned my head to look out the window again. I didn't want Brad to see how discouraged I was feeling.

The meadow was as lovely as I thought it would be. Tiny, bright wild flowers still bloomed. And the narrow brook was running sweetly over the stones. Just the way I'd pictured. But the rest?

Unpacking Brad's food, I placed it in the center of the blanket. As I did, garlic fumes rose into the warm air. I sat back on my heels and studied the arrangement. This lunch was not the one I'd planned when I'd first come up with the idea for our picnic.

Restaurant ham and cheese on rye, sitting on a paper napkin with The Copper Skillet printed on one corner, somehow couldn't compare favorably to a spread from a wicker basket that included a loaf of fresh french bread, imported cheese, grapes, and a sinfully rich chocolate dessert.

"Brad," I said, "I'm not all that hungry yet.

Why don't we take a walk first?" I looked around. "That looks pretty over there." I pointed to the edge of the woods where some large, purple wild flowers were nodding in the morning breeze. "If I remember right, I think there's a path over that way."

"Why not?" Jumping up, Brad held out a hand to help me up. He was still trying so hard to please me.

I took his hand, and we started across the meadow. Halfway to the woods, Brad tripped on something hidden in the grass and nearly fell. A look of annoyance briefly crossed his face before he could stop himself.

He really is miserable, I decided. And along with that realization came another. *I am, too.*

"Brad!" I turned so I could take his other hand. We stood facing each other in the knee-high grass. "Brad, I think it's time we were honest with each other."

"Honest?"

"Yes," I said softly. "All week you've tried to be different, to be the person you thought I wanted you to be. And I really appreciate the effort. But I want you to stop. Right now! I want you to go back to being the real you. No one should have to change themselves into someone they aren't."

"Am I really that transparent?"

"Completely," I answered.

"I'm sorry," he said, looking away.

"Don't be," I said. "Because your doing it made me realize I'd been doing the same thing. Trying to make myself over to please you. Patty saw what I was doing and tried to tell me how wrong I was being. But I wouldn't listen. I wanted your love too much."

"Deena, you have it," Brad assured me.

"No, not really," I answered. "I don't think you know the real me. And that isn't your fault. I never let you see the real me."

Brad shook his head with confusion.

"Brad!" My mouth was beginning to feel dry. I wanted to hurry and get this over with. "What would you say if I told you I never wanted to take the business courses that I signed up for? What if I told you I hated it every time you started talking about business? I would stop listening and start thinking of things like my current art project."

"Deena—" Brad started to say, looking hurt.

"I'm sorry," I broke in. "I don't mean to hurt you. But I have to tell you the truth. I've kept it to myself far too long." I squeezed Brad's hands, just to show him I still cared. But not the way I used to. "Not only do I hate business, I can't imagine myself ever wanting to be a part of that world. All I want out of life

141

is to be a good commercial artist. Maybe I'll starve. I don't know. But I do know this. It's the only way I'm ever going to be happy."

"Oh, Deena." Brad's look of pain had gradually changed to one of incredulity. "Why didn't you ever tell me this before?"

I nodded. "I should have." I smiled apologetically. "One more thing. If I win the art contest for the internship at an advertising agency this summer, I'm going to grab it."

"Deena," Brad shook his head again. "I don't know what to say. You surprise me."

"I know." I nodded. "Sometimes I surprise myself. I never thought I'd have the nerve to tell you what I just did."

"You needed *nerve* to talk to me?" Brad looked astonished.

"Yes." I looked him in the eyes. "You're so different from me, so practical and mature. I guess I was nervous that you wouldn't like me for the real me."

"Oh, Deena. I really am sorry. I'm sorry that I made you want to change. And I apologize for trying to get you to take classes you didn't want to take." He made a face. "I still don't think much of your idea of wanting to starve just to be an artist. I don't think I'll ever understand that kind of thinking. If it's what you want, though, then I guess you should have it."

"Thank you for understanding, Brad," I said. Suddenly, impulsively, I raised myself on my toes and kissed his cheek. "Now, why don't we pack up the picnic lunch and go home?" I grinned, trying to lighten the mood. "The ants have probably found it by now, anyway. And you told me that insects are one of your least favorite things on a picnic."

Driving back along the road to Pinebrook, we were both silent. I wasn't sure what was going through Brad's mind, but I was going over what I'd said out in the meadow.

I'd ruined the day for Brad. And I felt guilty about the things I'd said. But after a few miles I began to realize that I'd done the right thing. The truth had to come out sometime. If I'd lead Brad on, it would have been worse. He could have ended up hating me. And I didn't want that. This way, we were still friends.

I glanced over at his profile. It was a handsome profile. He wouldn't be alone for long. There were lots of nice girls in Pinebrook who would love to go out with him. I could think of one girl in particular.

"Brad," I broke into his silence. "You know something?" He looked over, frowning a little. "I know I'm the wrong girl for you." I smiled. "But I think I might know who *is* right for you. I think you probably already know, too. You simply haven't admitted it to yourself." I took a breath. "I think you and Tabitha Wingford would make the perfect couple."

"No," Brad denied. "No, Deena. You're wrong." And shaking his head, he fell silent again.

A few minutes later, his face had taken on a thoughtful look. I thought to myself that those thoughts probably included Tabitha.

Chapter Fifteen

I sat on the grassy knoll, overlooking the runway where Rick and I had shared hamburgers to celebrate my first official landing. That had been the beginning of our relationship. So it seemed appropriate to spend a few minutes there, saying goodbye to him. My knees were pulled up, my arms wrapped tightly around them. Tears streamed down my face.

Life was absolutely horrible.

I'd lost the art contest. And now I'd lost Rick.

From down at the opposite end of the runway, I heard the sound of a small plane run-up, getting ready to take off. Lifting my head, I brushed away enough tears so I could watch the plane lift off. I couldn't see it yet; it was still behind some buildings. But in a few seconds it would come rolling into sight, gather speed, and then lift off.

The plane came into view. My heart thumped and turned over as I recognized the sleek, shiny white painted sides and red racing stripes of *Quack-Quack*. As the plane rose into the air, flying low over my head, I caught only a brief glimpse of the dark-haired pilot. Had he turned at the last moment to look down? Had he seen me sitting there?

I watched as the plane banked and then continued to ascend. I watched until it became a tiny dot in the distance, then disappeared altogether. It was the last I would ever see of Rick Gillian.

Never again would I sit in that cockpit with him. Never again would we laugh together over some dumb thing I'd done while learning to fly. Never again would he compliment me on something I'd done right. Never again would he kiss me.

And it was my fault. I had no one to blame but my own childish self. Now that our argument was over and I'd cooled down, I knew that what Rick had said had been right. I couldn't believe that I'd acted the way I had, screaming at Rick, taking out my frustrations on him, telling him I never wanted to see him again.

We'd been standing on the tarmac near

the plane, going over the preflight checklist just as we'd done before all my lessons.

I wasn't paying attention to what I was doing. Twice Rick had gently reminded me to do something I'd overlooked. My answer had been to glower at him. Where was his sensitivity? Couldn't he see I was hurting? I didn't care about the oil level on a dipstick. That I hadn't yet told him about my losing the ad agency contest didn't really matter. He should have realized something terrible was wrong. He should have made me tell him and then taken me into his arms to console me. But, no, he just continued to walk around the plane, pulling at this, checking that. It was my third huge sigh that finally got to him.

"OK, Deena," he said with resignation. He leaned against the side of the plane, his arms folded. "If you've got a problem, spit it out. Did you have a flat tire this morning? Did you burn your breakfast toast? Did you run out of shampoo? What? Because your lack of attention to what you're doing is definitely the wrong attitude to take up in the sky with you. I thought I'd managed to impress that fact on you the first lesson. Or weren't you paying attention then, either?"

I could only blink at him for a second, trying to think how to respond. How could he possibly think I could be so unhappy and miserable over a flat tire or a burned piece of toast? I suddenly realized how little Rick must really know, or care, about me if he could think what he thought. "It's a little more serious than running out of shampoo," I said. "It just so happens I lost a contest. A very important contest. One I worked very hard to win."

"What was so important about it?" Rick asked, sounding a little concerned.

"The prize was an internship with an ad agency this summer. I would have had a chance to work for the entire summer in a real agency. It would have been a start on my career as a commercial artist."

"Hmmm." Rick cocked his head to one side and looked thoughtfully. "Well, Deena, I'm really sorry you lost. But do you think acting this way is really helping?"

"But I lost out to a guy who did his campaign on disposable diapers." Why couldn't he understand?

"And you don't think disposable diapers are important?"

"I don't believe you!" I yelled. I found myself practically screaming at him. "How stupid can you be? The product isn't the point at all. It was talent and execution of the artwork that counted."

Rick shifted his position and looked down at his feet. He was trying to maintain his cool despite my outburst. And that made me want to find something to throw at him.

Finally he looked up. "I'm only trying to help you see this in the right perspective, Deena. I can see how important winning was to you. But you're making yourself miserable by dwelling on the fact that you lost. And I hate to see you do that. So I wish you'd stop it." He ran his hand over his hair. "Look, I admit that I don't know anything about advertising. But there must be lots of other contests in the field. Why don't—"

"Oh, will you stop!" I spat out. "The last thing I need is your very adult advice. I've already had enough of that from my art teacher and my parents. I expected something different from you."

"Like what?" Rick's face was cloudy with confusion.

He didn't see what I wanted, him to hold me, comfort me, tell me everything would be all right. I wanted him to say that the judges had made a terrible mistake and that on Monday morning Mr. Lander would tell me I was the real winner. A sob caught at the back of my throat. But I *wasn't* the real winner, I thought. And life wasn't a romance novel.

"Oh, forget it," I said. "Let's just finish checking out the stupid plane so I can take my stupid lesson."

"I'll tell you what is stupid, Deena. Your thinking you're going to fly today. The lesson's canceled." The confused look was gone from Rick's face, replaced by one that was very serious.

"*What?*" I stared at him.

"You heard me." I could see his chest moving up and down. He was breathing hard. "You aren't fit to fly."

"Oh, really?"

"Absolutely!"

"Well, in that case, why not cancel any future lessons, too?" I said, while a little voice in the back of my head was saying, "Deena, what are you doing?" I could see Rick's look change again. Was it hurt or astonishment? "And while we're at it, why not cancel our relationship as well? Because, quite frankly, I don't think I ever want to see you again."

I turned and stormed away in the direction of the parking lot. I'd lost control completely.

I didn't even get to my car before I wanted to run back to apologize to Rick. But I didn't. I couldn't. How could I go back and face him after all those horrible things I'd said and the way I'd acted? So I'd come here, to the grassy knoll. And I'd seen Rick fly away, out of my life.

I cried, knowing Rick was right and being unable to tell him. There *would* be other contests. There would be other chances to show off my talent, to prove to myself and others that I would someday make a good—no, terrific—commercial artist. I just wished that—"

"Deena!" It was Rick's voice.

Startled, I swung my head around. "Rick?"

"That's me." Rick's mouth turned up in a tentative smile.

I shook my head. "I saw you take off. I mean, wasn't that you in *Quack-Quack* a few minutes ago?"

"Yes." Rick nodded. "But when I saw you sitting down here, I came back and landed."

"Oh," I said softly. For a moment I wasn't sure what to say next. Then I knew. "Rick," I said, looking up into his dark eyes, "I'm sorry. You were right. Everything you said was right. But I was acting like a baby and wouldn't listen."

"And I was acting like an idiot," Rick answered. "I was trying so hard to prove what an adult I was, giving you advice when what you needed was a sympathetic shoulder. I almost blew what we were beginning to build together." All at once he was next to me, reaching down to take my hands and pull me to my feet so that I was standing close to him.

"Are you saying," I asked, "that you forgive the dumb way I acted?"

"Only," Rick said, putting his arms gently around my shoulders, "if you forgive the dumb way I acted."

"And if you'll keep on giving me lessons."

"As long as you want me to," Rick said, tilting my face upward and kissing me.

The feeling I had at that moment was like only one other thing in this world—flying.

We hope you enjoyed reading this book. All the titles currently available in the Sweet Dreams series are listed on page two. They are all available at your local bookshop or newsagent, though should you find any difficulty in obtaining the books you would like, you can order direct from the publisher, at the address below. Also, if you would like to know more about the series, or would simply like to tell us what you think of the series, write to:

Kim Prior,
Sweet Dreams,
Transworld Publishers Limited,
61–63 Uxbridge Road,
London W5 5SA.

To order books, please list the title(s) you would like, and send together with your name and address, and a cheque or postal order made payable to TRANSWORLD PUBLISHERS LIMITED. Please allow cost of book(s) plus 20p for the first book and 10p for each additional book for postage and packing.

(The above applies to readers in the UK and Ireland only.)

If you live in Australia or New Zealand, and would like more information about the series, please write to:

Sally Porter,
Sweet Dreams
Corgi & Bantam Books,
26 Harley Crescent,
Condell Park,
N.S.W. 2200,
Australia.

Kiri Martin
Sweet Dreams
c/o Corgi & Bantam Books
  New Zealand,
Cnr. Moselle and Waipareira
  Avenues,
Henderson,
Auckland,
New Zealand.

If you enjoy Sweet Dreams, there's a whole series of books you'll like just as much!

SWEET VALLEY HIGH

Created by Francine Pascal
Written by Kate William

SWEET VALLEY HIGH is a great series of books about identical twins, Elizabeth and Jessica Wakefield, and all their friends at Sweet Valley High. The twins are popular, daring and smart – but Jessica is always scheming and plotting in ways only she knows how, leaving Elizabeth to sort out the mess!

Every story is an exciting insight into the lives of the Sweet Valley High 'gang' – and every one ends on a gripping cliffhanger!

So come and join the Wakefield twins and share in their many adventures!

Here's a list of all the Sweet Valley High titles currently available in the shops:

SWEET VALLEY HIGH SUPER SPECIALS

CW00499595

Retired

NOT EXPIRED

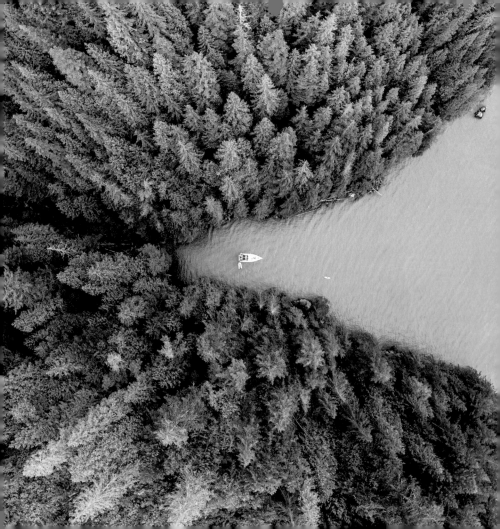

▣ WILLOW CREEK PRESS®

Published by Willow Creek Press, Inc.
P.O. Box 147, Minocqua, Wisconsin 54548

All Photos © Shutterstock

Printed in China

Find Joy in the Journey.

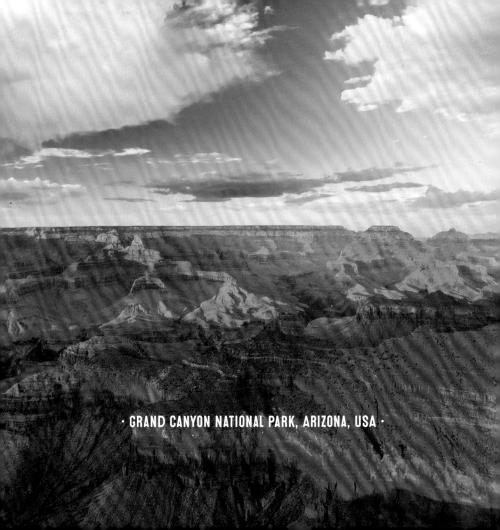

· GRAND CANYON NATIONAL PARK, ARIZONA, USA ·

"THERE IS A WHOLE NEW KIND OF LIFE AHEAD, FULL OF EXPERIENCES JUST WAITING TO HAPPEN. SOME CALL IT 'RETIREMENT.' I CALL IT BLISS."

-BETTY SULLIVAN

"IT IS NEVER TOO
LATE TO BE WHO YOU
MIGHT HAVE BEEN."

-GEORGE ELIOT

· BACHALPSEE LAKE, SWITZERLAND ·

· MEALT FALLS, SCOTLAND ·

Musings

WRITE YOUR LIFE STORY IN REVERSE. What are the things that you want to be able to say that you did?

. . . .

"RETIREMENT, A TIME TO
ENJOY ALL THE THINGS
YOU NEVER HAD TIME TO
DO WHEN YOU WORKED."

-CATHERINE PULSIFER

· CASTIGLIONE FALLETTO, ITALY ·

· SONORAN DESERT, ARIZONA, USA ·

"THE BEST WAY TO PAY
FOR A LOVELY MOMENT
IS TO ENJOY IT."

-RICHARD BACH

"A LOT OF OUR FRIENDS COMPLAIN ABOUT THEIR RETIREMENT.

We tell 'em
to get a life."

–LARRY LASER

· SINIS PENINSULA, SARDINIA, ITALY ·

· COLORADO, USA ·

"NOTHING EVER
BECOMES REAL TILL IT
IS EXPERIENCED."

-JOHN KEATS

"THE BIGGEST
ADVENTURE YOU CAN
EVER TAKE IS TO LIVE THE
LIFE OF YOUR DREAMS."

-OPRAH WINFREY

· ALGARVE, PORTUGAL ·

RETIREMENT BLUES

These longevity havens, known as blue zones, are known for their populations of long-lived, healthy elders.

· OGLIASTRA REGION, SARDINIA ·

· LOMA LINDA, CALIFORNIA ·

· IKARIA, GREECE ·

· NICOYA PENINSULA, COSTA RICA ·

AGE IS JUST A LEVEL
IN THE GAME OF LIFE.

People in these communities tend to incorporate natural physical movement each day, wake up with a purpose, find time to decompress, lean on a plant-forward diet, belong to a faith, put family first, and stay connected with a social circle of friends.

· OKINAWA, JAPAN ·

"TELL ME, WHAT IS IT
YOU PLAN TO DO WITH
YOUR ONE WILD AND
PRECIOUS LIFE?"

-MARY OLIVER

· HUBBARD GLACIER, ALASKA, USA ·

· PROVENCE, FRANCE ·

"WE ARE NOT HUMAN
BEINGS HAVING A
SPIRITUAL EXPERIENCE.
WE ARE SPIRITUAL
BEINGS HAVING A
HUMAN EXPERIENCE."

-PIERRE TEILHARD DE CHARDIN

"I ENJOY WAKING UP AND NOT HAVING TO GO TO WORK.

THAILAND

SO I DO IT
three or four
TIMES A DAY."

-GENE PERRET

· MONUMENT VALLEY, ARIZONA, USA ·

"IT'S NOT THE DAYS IN
LIFE WE REMEMBER,
RATHER THE MOMENTS."

-WALT DISNEY

"GETTING OLD IS LIKE
CLIMBING A MOUNTAIN;
YOU GET A LITTLE OUT
OF BREATH, BUT THE
VIEW IS MUCH BETTER!"

-INGRID BERGMAN

· MALETSUNYANE FALLS, AFRICA ·

· SKOGAR, ICELAND ·

Musings

FOCUS ON GRATITUDE.
If you woke up tomorrow
and only had the things you
were grateful for today,
what would they be?

....

"HUMANS ARE SOCIAL
BEINGS, AND WE ARE
HAPPIER, AND BETTER,
WHEN CONNECTED TO
OTHERS."

-PAUL BLOOM

SANTORINI, GREECE ·

· LEUCHTTURM LIST-OST, GERMANY ·

"THERE ARE TWO WAYS OF SPREADING LIGHT. TO BE THE CANDLE OR THE MIRROR THAT REFLECTS IT."

-EDITH WHARTON

"RETIRE FROM WORK, BUT NOT *from life*."

—M.K. SONI

· FINLAND ·

STRYN, NORWAY

"NO MAN EVER STEPS IN
THE SAME RIVER TWICE,
FOR IT'S NOT THE SAME
RIVER AND HE'S NOT THE
SAME MAN."

-HERACLITUS

"A JOURNEY OF A
THOUSAND MILES BEGINS
WITH A SINGLE STEP."

-LAO TZU

· APPALACHIAN TRAIL, USA ·

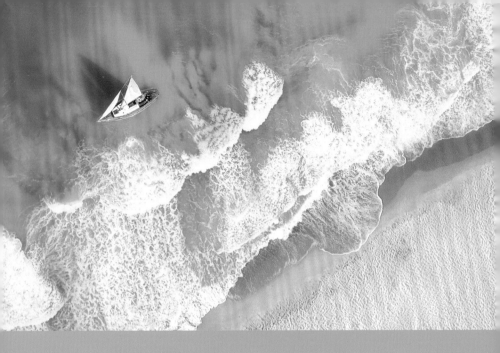

Make Hobbies a Habit

Hobbies serve as an excellent form of self-care by improving cognitive function and memory, encouraging relaxation, providing opportunities for achievement and recognition, promoting social connectedness, and reducing loneliness and isolation.

Acting	Genealogy	Quilting
Antiquing	Geocaching	Reading
Archery	Ghost Hunting	Rock Climbing
Baking	Golf	Sailing
Beekeeping	Hiking	Scrapbooking
Biking	Home Brewing	Singing
Bird Watching	Investment	Skydiving
Calligraphy	Leather Crafting	Spelunking
Citizen Scientist	Magic	Stand-Up Comedy
Coloring	Martial Arts	Stargazing
Cooking	Meditation	Swimming
Crochet	Mentoring	Tai Chi
Cross-Stitching	Mixology	Train Spotting
Dancing	Origami	Travel
Dragon Boat Racing	Painting	Upcycling
Fishing	Philosophy	Volunteering
Foraging	Photography	Walking
Foreign Language	Pickleball	Woodworking
Gaming	Play an Instrument	Writing
Gardening	Pottery	Yoga

"LIFE IS LIKE RIDING
A BICYCLE. TO KEEP
YOUR BALANCE, YOU
MUST KEEP MOVING."

-ALBERT EINSTEIN

· TUSCANY, ITALY ·

"THERE'S NEVER
ENOUGH TIME TO DO
ALL THE NOTHING
YOU WANT."

-BILL WATTERSON

CALA GOLORITZE, SARDINIA, ITALY

"TOO MUCH
OF A GOOD
THING CAN BE
wonderful!"

—MAE WEST

· DISKO BAY, GREENLAND ·

"EMBRACE UNCERTAINTY.
SOME OF THE MOST
BEAUTIFUL CHAPTERS IN
OUR LIVES WON'T HAVE A
TITLE UNTIL MUCH LATER."

-BOB GOFF

"THERE ARE FAR
BETTER THINGS
AHEAD THAN
WE EVER LEAVE
BEHIND."

-C.S. LEWIS

ZION NATIONAL PARK, UTAH, USA

· KIRKJUFELLSFOSS, ICELAND ·

Musings

JOY IS EASIER THAN HAPPINESS. What was the last thing you saw that brought you joy?

....

"BETWEEN THE WISH
AND THE THING
THE WORLD LIES
WAITING."

-CORMAC MCCARTHY

PARIS, FRANCE

· PATAGONIA, CHILE ·

"LIFE IS THE ART OF
DRAWING WITHOUT
AN ERASER."

-JOHN W. GARDNER

· KVARNER GULF, CROATIA ·

"THE MOST IMPORTANT THING IS TO *enjoy your life.*"

-AUDREY HEPBURN

"NOW IS NO TIME TO
THINK OF WHAT YOU DO
NOT HAVE. THINK OF
WHAT YOU CAN DO WITH
WHAT THERE IS."

-ERNEST HEMINGWAY

"OFTEN WHEN YOU THINK
YOU'RE AT THE END OF
SOMETHING, YOU'RE
AT THE BEGINNING OF
SOMETHING ELSE."

-FRED ROGERS

· MUSKEGON, MICHIGAN, USA ·

HAKUNA MATATA
· *Africa* ·
NO PROBLEM,
NO WORRIES

LAGOM
· *Sweden* ·
NOT TOO MUCH,
NOT TOO LITTLE

GEZELLIG
· *Netherlands* ·
SOCIAL COZINESS

AYLYAK
· *Bulgaria* ·
A RELAXED PACE
WITHOUT WORRY

TRI HITA KARANA
· *Bali* ·
BE IN HARMONY
WITH PEOPLE,
GOD, & NATURE

JOIE DE VIVRE
· *France* ·
JOY OF LIVING

MERAKI
· *Greece* ·
DOING SOMETHING WITH
YOUR ENTIRE SOUL

FRILUFTSLIV
· *Norway* ·
OPEN-AIR LIVING

HYGGE
· *Denmark* ·
COMFORTABLE
CONVIVIALITY

COSAGACH
· *Scotland* ·
SNUG & SHELTERED

DOLCE FAR NIENTE
· *Italy* ·
SWEET DOING NOTHING

FERNWEH
· *Germany* ·
WANDERLUST OR
A DESIRE TO TRAVEL

IKIGAI
· *Japan* ·
YOUR REASON
FOR BEING

find your
philosophy

UBUNTU
· *Africa* ·
I AM BECAUSE WE ARE

PURA VIDA
· *Costa Rica* ·
FOCUS ON GRATITUDE.
TAKE IT EASY.
HUMILITY IS STRENGTH

WABI-SABI
· *Japan* ·
ACCEPT IMPERFECTION

"LIFE CAN ONLY
BE UNDERSTOOD
BACKWARDS; BUT
IT MUST BE LIVED
FORWARDS."

-SOREN KIERKEGAARD

· WASHINGTON MONUMENT, WASHINGTON, D.C., USA ·

· NEUSCHWANSTEIN CASTLE, GERMANY ·

"IT IS BETTER TO
LIVE RICH THAN
TO DIE RICH."

-SAMUEL JOHNSON

"IT'S TIME TO SAY *goodbye*, BUT I THINK GOODBYES ARE SAD

· BLUE RIDGE PARKWAY, NORTH CAROLINA, USA ·

AND I'D MUCH RATHER SAY *hello*. HELLO TO A NEW ADVENTURE."

-ERNIE HARWELL

· CAPE COD, MASSACHUSETTS, USA ·

"FOR MANY, RETIREMENT IS A TIME FOR PERSONAL GROWTH, WHICH BECOMES THE PATH TO GREATER FREEDOM."

-ROBERT DELAMONTAGNE

"HALF OUR LIFE IS
SPENT TRYING TO FIND
SOMETHING TO DO WITH
THE TIME WE HAVE
RUSHED THROUGH LIFE
TRYING TO SAVE."

-WILL ROGERS

· GLENFINNAN VIADUCT, SCOTLAND ·

· MALIGNE LAKE, JASPER NATIONAL PARK, CANADA ·

Musings

EMBRACE WANDERLUST.

If you could snap
your fingers and be
somewhere else instantly,
where would you go?

. . . .

"IT'S NOT WHAT
YOU LOOK AT THAT
MATTERS, IT'S
WHAT YOU SEE."

-HENRY DAVID THOREAU

· ARCHES NATIONAL PARK, UTAH, USA ·

· BIG SUR, CALIFORNIA, USA ·

"JUST LIVING IS NOT ENOUGH... ONE MUST HAVE SUNSHINE, FREEDOM, AND A LITTLE FLOWER."

-HANS CHRISTIAN ANDERSEN

· OKINAWA, JAPAN ·

"THERE'S A *whole world* OUT THERE, RIGHT OUTSIDE YOUR WINDOW. YOU'D BE A FOOL TO MISS IT."

—CHARLOTTE ERIKSSON

· SEYCHELLES ·

"IN ALL OF LIVING,
HAVE MUCH FUN AND
LAUGHTER. LIFE IS
TO BE ENJOYED, NOT
JUST ENDURED."

–GORDON B. HINCKLEY

"YOU ARE NOT WITHDRAWING FROM LIFE; YOU ARE REDRAWING YOUR LIFE."

-NEALE GODFREY

· BARCELONA, SPAIN ·

OLYMPIC NATIONAL PARK, WASHINGTON, USA ·

"TO ME, RETIREMENT
MEANS DOING WHAT YOU
HAVE FUN DOING."

-DICK VAN DYKE

· GREAT SMOKY MOUNTAINS NATIONAL PARK, TENNESSEE, USA ·

There's life and then there's the good life.